# THE TREE THAT STOOD STILL

## AMRA PAJALIĆ

# 1-Dawn

Zora and I ran up the hill behind our houses, my calves aching, my chest tight as the hill got steeper and steeper. Zora was fleet-footed before me, taking long strides thanks to her tall and lean frame. She was a runner with much better stamina. She disappeared among the foliage while I laboriously continued my trek, perspiring from the warmth of the spring sunshine. As I climbed, I eyed the trees for movement.

"Rah," Zora jumped out from a bush and screamed.

I didn't flinch.

I smiled as she screamed in frustration behind me. She loved scaring me, but after being best friends for most of our fifteen years she was losing her touch, or maybe I was building up a better tolerance.

We reached the clearing where we played, near our favourite tree. As I ran, my coin necklace bounced hard against my collarbone. I quickly tucked it under my shirt. Babo bought me the Tito coin at a market in Vukovar. They made the silver coin to commemorate President Tito's death on the 4th of May 1980, which was also the date of my birthday, even though I was born three years before Tito died. I used to carry the coin in my pocket, but one day, I lost it at school. After spending all of lunch looking for it so my brother made a hole in the coin and threaded a necklace that Mama gave him.

I reached Ćelo in record time, panting from running up the hill. Ćelo, meaning baldie, was a birch tree that Zora named because the branches were so full and luscious, using the nickname her father used for his work buddy at the mines. When Zora asked her father why he was called his workmate Ćelo even though he had a full head of hair, her father told her that his work friends thought it was funny to give a nickname that was opposite to his actual trait.

I sat on a log from a fallen branch and got my breath back, while Zora bounded in carrying a wild white orchid in her hand, her blue skirt swaying, her short ash-blonde hair glinting in the dappled sunshine breaking through the birch trees around us. She handed me the white flower. It contrasted with the olive-tinged skin of my hand, an inheritance from my Ottoman ancestry. I smelled its sweet scent and tucked it into her hair above her ear as her brilliant blue eyes watched me.

Zora and I stubbornly stuck together, excluding the other children in our neighbourhood who tried to play with us. Among the trees and thickets of blackberries, we took turns pretending to be Robin Hood and Marion or Jasmine and Aladdin when we were younger. We swapped the male and female roles, even though Zora made a better boy with her short blonde hair and her peaches and cream skin, while my long brown hair suited the role of a maiden in distress. The story always ended with the lovers being reunited, Zora and I ending our game in a lip-smacking kiss, keeping our lips closed. The other children always tried to change our games into war games, or hide and seek, but we were only interested in our romance stories.

I took the romance novel from my backpack and opened the page. We could only read here in the trees. Zora's house was full. She was the middle of five siblings, so someone always followed us around, or bossed us at her house.

My mother would punish me if she knew I was taking her books. She kept them hidden in a cupboard in her bedroom to read at night before bed. We came to our secret spot to read the books, especially the kissing and making love parts, attempting to decipher the flowery language that described lovemaking.

*He tensed beneath her touch, taking hold of her hands, holding them against his chest. She kept her eyes closed, waiting for a kiss.*

As I read, my voice cracked. Zora snorted with laughter.

*The moment stretched out; she opened her eyes and frowned. Tristan's hard jaw was just above her face.*

Zora was looking dreamy-eyed into the distance. "Do you think we'll find a love like that?" she asked.

I considered the boys we knew, picturing them in place of Tristan. "Not with the boys in our class," I muttered.

Zora burst out laughing. I laughed with her. I returned the book to my backpack.

Zora glanced at her watch. "We'd better get going," she said.

I stood, putting on my backpack. We clambered back down the steep hill, the green canopy of the conifer and birch trees looking like green fairy floss, the burgundy terracotta tile roofs of the white-rendered houses peeking through the foliage.

The main road stretched in the valley between steep hills, like a long, thin finger that was dotted with houses and buildings.

We walked the steep, curving road toward the centre of town and our high school. We were on afternoon shift, which began at one p.m. and finished at six p.m. The schoolhouse was a three-storey square white building that abutted a hill with the forest framing it from behind. The conifer trees were spiky and unruly as they covered the hill. I walked beside Zora onto the basketball court in front of the school, through the carpark, entering the front doorway. I climbed up the stairs to the third storey while students streamed ahead of us. The corridors echoed with the chatter, and the squeaky shoes on linoleum filled the air.

I followed Zora into our classroom, the thick and dusty smell of chalk enveloping me. Mrs Tanović was already at her desk in the corner near the chalkboard. She was wearing her glasses as she paged through *The Catcher in the Rye*, peering over the edge to see who was entering. Zora and I took our usual seats by the windows and opened our books, preparing for the first lesson of the day.

It was our first year of high school. Zora and I attended the same primary school and risked being separated if we wanted to study different pathways. My father attempted to talk me into going to the mechanical high school so I would be an engineer, but I insisted on going to the veterinarian high school with Zora. For the first two years of high school we would study general subjects, then in years three and four we would study subjects to prepare us for a veterinarian univer-sity in Belgrade. We'd already planned out our lives; Zora and I would go to university together in Belgrade, the capital city of Serbia, which was two hours away, and when we returned, we would open a practice together. We already had a name, A New Dawn, inspired by Zora's first name, which meant dawn.

The bell went at one pm. The classroom was half empty, and empty desks surrounded me. I pictured the students who were supposed to be sitting in them, their names bouncing through my head, and a dangerous thought erupted. They were all Serbs. I pushed the thought away.

Mrs Tanović stood at the front and waited. She peered at the classroom door, but no one else entered. "We should begin," she said.

I looked at Zora with concern. Every day, the classroom was getting emptier and emptier. I tore out a sheet of paper and folded it into strips.

*Why is everyone leaving?* I wrote and passed the note to Zora when the teacher turned her back to us to write on the board. Dust particles from the chalk floating in the surrounding air, filtered by beams of light from the window.

Zora quickly scribbled and handed it back to me. *Don't know.*

I copied down the teacher's notes, Zora's face giving me pause. It was almost as if she were uncomfortable with my question, but how could that be? We told each other everything, always.

At the end of the day, Zora went to the toilet while I went to the library to return a book. I read a few pages of my book as I waited for her in front of the library. After a few minutes, when she wasn't appearing down the corridor, I headed down the stairs to the toilet. I saw the classroom bully and his friends huddled in a corner. Zora and I called him Toaster Head because his head was square like a toaster on his thick neck. I walked toward them and saw Zora's golden hair over their shoulders.

"Why haven't you left like the other Serbs?" Toaster Head shouted as I approached.

"Why would she leave?" I lifted my backpack, hitting Toaster Head in the back with it.

He turned, his fists clenched. Seeing it was me, he put his fists down. "You need to pick better friends, Torlak." He gestured to his friends, and they swaggered down the corridor.

"You need to pick on someone your own size, you coward," I shouted.

Toaster Head stopped and turned to face me. Zora grabbed my arm, pushing me behind her.

"You'd better watch your back, Torlak. We need to stick together." He turned and left.

"Are you okay?" I asked while we walked home.

"Of course." Zora didn't look at me.

"You can tell me anything, you know. I don't care what that idiot said. You and I are on the same side."

Zora nodded but said nothing. We'd been best friends for too long, and I knew when not to push with questions.

When we arrived at our house, our fathers were sitting at a table under the grapevine frame in Zora's front yard, sipping *rakija*, plum brandy, that Zora's father Slobodan made from his plum trees. Slobodan was wearing his grey mining overalls, a red indent from his hard hat along his hairline, his black hair matted against his head, and his black bushy beard covering his face. He was a miner in the bauxite mines on the southern edge of our town. He was gesticulating with his hands, his face flushed, and his voice booming.

"Fadil, you can't let these idiots dictate to us our lives."

Zora and I ducked behind the plum trees so that we were unseen. Yugoslavia has been experiencing unrest for the past few months. Slovenia and Croatia were the first republics that voted for independence away from the Federation of Yugoslavia that was created by President Tito after World War II. This led to a ten-day war between the two former republics. Bosnia and Hercegovina voted for independence, and suddenly, they replaced all the photos of President Tito in public buildings with Alija Izetbegović, the Bosnian President.

Mama took down Tito's photo in our living room, leaving a bright white patch on the wall that was protected from Babo's cigarette smoke. When Babo came home from work, he'd returned it and told her not to buy into the nationalistic nonsense that the politicians were propagating. He said that Bosnia was always a multiethnic melting pot with minorities of Serbs and Croatians. It was the Serbian nationalist government who wanted to take Bosnia's territory, and we should not let them incite us.

Soon after, the Serbian government used blockades to create shortages of food and petrol supplies. We'd been caught off guard by the blockade, using up our supplies within a week. Babo travelled to the village to collect jars of preserves and frozen vegetables that my grandparents harvested and stored. Every summer, my grandparents picked fruit from their trees, pears, apples, peaches, and cherries, and preserved them by cooking them for hours on the stove with sugar and storing the fruit in glass jars. They also owned large plots of land around the house from which they harvested vegetables that they stockpiled in plastic bags in a large freezer in their hallway. My Nana slaughtered chickens, and they froze them too. The only things that my grandparents bought were sugar, salt and oil. Otherwise, they were totally self-sufficient, while in the city, we relied on buying everything we needed.

Afterwards, Babo hadn't been able to travel to work because we ran out of petrol, so he'd walked the seven kilometres on foot in each direction. His temper became explosive because of the cigarette shortage. During the economic blockade, Babo made do with the Drina cigarettes, which were manufactured in Sarajevo. He'd complained the whole time about their inferior quality. When the blockade lifted, he'd bought ten packs of cigarettes and hidden them throughout the house for a rainy day.

I hoped that the craziness ended, but it seemed things were only becoming worse with each passing day.

"I agree, Slobodan. We are one people," my father said, his voice defeated. It surprised me that he was home so early. Despite being an engineer at the aluminium mine in Potočari, they drafted him to become a member of a delegation with Serbs and Bosnians, who were negotiating a power-sharing arrangement. Every day for the past week, he travelled on a bus to Bratunac, a town that was 11 kilometres away, and then drove to work afterwards. He came home late at night, sometimes even after I was asleep. He'd said that the delegation was an opportunity for a peaceful solution to the unrest, but now he sounded doubtful.

"Brotherhood and unity need to prevail." My father rolled the shot glass in his hands. He was a fervent communist and believed in the ideals of brotherhood and unity over ethnic lines. "The Serbs say that if they don't get Potočari, they will stop negotiations."

Potočari was a village two miles north of Srebrenica. It was where the Yugoslav Communist government built a car battery, car brake, and zinc processing factories. The silver mines, which gave our town its name, were situated in Potočari. Additionally, it now hosted bauxite and zinc mines. This was where Babo and most of the residents of Srebrenica worked and why he called it the 'life's blood of Srebrenica.' It was the mining and factory jobs that ensured that men from Srebrenica didn't have to leave to work abroad or in neighbouring cities, and that guaranteed everyone such a good life. Babo bragged to my uncle in Australia that we, too, lived like in the West and owned a car and a house and that we were building a summer cottage.

I reached for Zora's hand and gripped it. Our families were intertwined as if we were related. We spent many evenings and days together. When my family celebrated Ramadan, we invited her family. When Zora's family celebrated Orthodox Christmas, they invited us, and we celebrated New Year and communist events together. Nothing divided us. We were the one people, and yet now we were being told that we were not. That somehow we differed from each other.

"What are they playing at?" Slobodan said. "Who wants a war? You are more of a brother to me than my own biological brother." He shook his head, his elbows on the table as he slumped forward and held his head in his hands.

"I know, Slobo, I know." My father slugged back another shot. "I'd better go see Esma and the kids." He rose and patted

Slobodan on the back. Slobodan patted my father's hand. He poured himself another shot while my father entered our house.

"See you tomorrow." Zora quickly brushed her lips against my cheek before walking down the plum-lined path to her house.

Usually we lingered, talking and laughing, but a pall hung over us.

When I entered my house, my mother was serving dinner, wearing a dark blue skirt and white shirt with a matching dark blue vest. She worked in the office at the same mine as my father. The two of them met on the job twenty years before.

"Seka, call your brother," Mama said.

I climbed up the stairs, threw my schoolbag into my room, and knocked on Emir's door. When he didn't answer, I pushed open the door. He was lying on his bed in a t-shirt and jeans. He tugged down the earphones of his Walkman and looked at me with annoyance in his brown eyes.

"What do you want?" he demanded.

"Mama is serving dinner."

He sat up, swinging his legs onto the floor of the bed and turning off the Walkman. He had been in a dark mood for the past few weeks, and I was the only one who knew why.

Last week, while I was watching television, my brother had rushed into the house and up the stairs. Mama was at the local shop buying groceries, Babo was at work.

I ran upstairs and to the bathroom. The bathroom was locked. After watching television, I came back and found it still locked.

"Emir, get out." I banged on the door. The toilet and the bathroom were in the same room.

"Go away, I'm busy," Emir shouted.

His voice sounded hoarse, like he had a cold. Mama told me that sometimes boys needed privacy in the bathroom and not to bother him. I gleaned from Zora, who had older brothers, what they were actually doing behind locked doors.

"Emir, hurry." I kept banging.

The door slammed open. Emir was bare-chested, with dark bruises on his arms in the shape of hands, a footprint on his chest. He had a cut lip, with droplets of blood seeping from the edges. He rushed past me and into his bedroom.

I ran into the bathroom, sighing with relief as I sat on the toilet. Emir's crumpled t-shirt was on the ground. I picked up the t-shirt and noticed that it was torn nearly in half. It was his favourite, Adidas. Our uncle, who worked in Germany, bought it for Emir, and my brother wore it nearly every day.

After I washed my hands, I knocked on his door. "Emir, I have your t-shirt."

He opened the door, snatching the t-shirt from my arms. I pushed myself into his room before he could close it in my face. "What happened? Were you in a fight?"

In the past few months, Emir surpassed my father's height. My mother said proudly that he took after her side of the family. All her brothers loomed like giants. Since he'd reached his height, Emir was getting into scraps at school, the other boys testing themselves against him, but the fighting never got bloody.

"I don't want to talk about it. Go away." He pushed me.

I grabbed the bed so I didn't fall. "I'm telling Babo on you." Babo told Emir if he got into any more fights, he would give him the beating he was asking for.

"Don't, please, Seka." Emir turned his face away, a tear dripping off his chin.

"What happened?" I placed my hand on his arm and sat on the bed next to him.

Emir was so strong, and I hadn't seen him cry. Not since he'd turned eighteen a few months ago and declared himself a man.

Emir told me he went to his favourite cafe after school to do his homework with his friends. Emir greeted the owner behind the counter, who didn't return his greeting while he served him his Coke. My brother was perturbed by the owner's chilly reception and was about to leave when a former student from his school came in with his friends, wearing a Metallica t-shirt. Metallica t-shirt was older than Emir and had graduated the year before, but they knew each other from the track field. They sat down together, reminiscing about their track field days.

"Do you want to go for a drive with us?" Metallica T-shirt asked.

Emir nodded with relief. He wondered what he did to receive such glowering stares from the owner and vowed not to return.

Metallica T-shirt drove and Emir was in the back, between two other boys.

"So, *Balija*, how do you like my car?" Metallica T-shirt asked.

Emir was thrown off kilter. He knew that *Balija* was a slur used against Muslims, but he'd never been called this.

"I'm not a *Balija*. I'm a Yugoslav, like you."

"You're nothing like me, Turk. Your people shed the blood of my people five centuries ago."

"What are you talking about?" Emir asked.

"The Battle of Kosovo when the Turks invaded our Serb motherland and subjugated my people."

"That was 500 years ago, and anyway, you're from Srebrenica, like me?"

"I am a Serb and you are a Turk. Now it's time for us to shed the blood of Turks."

Emir thought he was joking, but then the two boys sitting on each side of him exchanged the Serb salute, making a sign of the cross by holding their thumb and the index and middle fingers together. They punched him in the ribs. Emir fought back, but the small Fićo supermini car left him trapped with no space.

Metallica T-shirt turned off the main road and into a side street. He braked suddenly and turned in his seat, punching Emir in the stomach. Emir punched him back, landing a blow on Metallica T-shirt's chin.

"Get him out. I want him worked over good," Metallica T-shirt shouted, getting out of the car.

They yanked Emir from the car, and two boys held him while Metallica T-shirt and his friend from the passenger seat took turns punching him until he fell to the ground. One of them stomped on his chest.

A car stopped next to them. "What are you boys doing?" the male driver demanded as he peered out the window.

Metallica T-shirt punched Emir one last time and got in his car. "Stay out of our cafe, *Balija*." He drove off, spinning his wheels.

The driver got out of his car and helped Emir up. "I'll take you home."

Emir was hurting all over his torso. He sat in the passenger seat and wiped the blood from his split lip.

He made me promise not to tell our parents. He said our father had enough on his plate, and Mama would only worry. I let him persuade me it was better that no one knew but I was now regretting making my promise. It was like he was being corroded from the inside by battery acid, transforming into someone nasty and twisted. I wished I could talk to Zora about it, but we avoided talking about anything to do with the unrest.

I returned downstairs, and Emir followed. We ate dinner in a subdued silence. Mama kept glancing at my father with concern. He must have told her about the demands at the delegation and she was unsettled, too.

Afterwards, Emir and I went to our own bedrooms. I heard my parents talking downstairs and tiptoed to the top of the stairs to eavesdrop. A few minutes later, Emir carefully opened his door, tiptoeing barefoot to join me.

"We should go to my brother Merhad in Germany. Or Merima in Austria," Mama said.

Tightly, I squeezed the banister. I didn't want to leave my home, everything I knew. I glanced at Emir; he looked concerned too.

"We just finished building the house. And we bought the block of land for the summer house. Things will die down."

"Then let me take the children to my parents in Kobilja Glava," Mama said.

"Emir is in his last year of high school. We can't disrupt his final exams."

There was a knock at the front door. "Who could that be at ten o'clock at night?" Babo walked to the front door carrying his glass of *rakija,* disappearing from sight in the hallway. "Boris, what are you doing here? Come in. Come in."

Emir and I looked at each other with surprise. We visited Boris and his family regularly, but he wouldn't come to our house so late unless it was an emergency.

Boris stepped into the hallway, closing the door behind him. "I don't have much time. Snežana is packing, and we're leaving tonight."

"Where are you going?" Babo asked. "Do you want a *rakija?*"

Boris hesitated before quickly nodding.

Babo walked back to the living room. Mama already poured a shot glass for Boris, and Babo handed it to him.

Boris gulped the shot down. "We've been getting calls all night, every night. They're telling us we have to leave. That if we're true nationalists, we will join the winning side and help make a Greater Serbia. They say if we don't leave, they will kill us all."

"Who is making these crank calls? What idiots? Go to the police and have them deal with it."

From upstairs, we could hear the fear and desperation in his voice.

"They know my children's names. They know where they go to school. They know everything. I tried to stay. You know me, Fadil. I don't believe in all this nationalist nonsense. Brotherhood and Unity is my party, but I can't risk my children. I can't risk it."

"Of course, Boris." Babo patted him on the back. "Do you need anything?"

"Can you keep an eye on our house?" Boris asked. "I hope that all this will calm down in a few weeks, but for now, we're going to Snežana's family in Duboko. I called work and told them that Snežana's mother is sick. Please don't tell anyone the truth. I don't want anyone thinking that we're picking sides."

"I'll see you in a few weeks," Babo said, walking Boris out.

I took a step down and peered through the banister and saw Boris hesitate on the front porch before turning around and hugging Babo. "Take care of yourself, my friend."

"You too," Babo said. "You too." He remained in the doorway, watching Boris drive away.

Emir and I looked at each other with wide eyes, before quickly tiptoeing back to our rooms.

The next day I waited for Zora by my fence. I hadn't slept well, tossing and turning as I remembered Boris' fear. Was this why all the Serbs had left town? I finally understood Zora's tense face. When she arrived, we walked up the hill to our secret place. We sat at the base of the tree side by side. I took the romance novel out of my bag.

"I need to ask you something." I thumbed through the pages, finding where we stopped yesterday. "Are people calling you at night, telling your father he needs to fight for a Greater Serbia?"

Zora said nothing. From the corner of my eye, I saw her hands tighten on her knees, her head bow. I glanced over, and she was crying.

I hugged her tightly, dropping the book.

"I wanted to tell you," she whispered against my shoulder, "but I didn't want you to think we were like them. In the beginning, my father would argue with them, and then hang up. Now he leaves the phone off the hook."

"I don't want you to leave." I hugged her tighter to me, my tears streaming into her hair.

"I don't want to either. I want everything to go back to normal."

"It will." I cleared my throat. "Everything will be as it once was."

Zora patted my hand but said nothing. We looked at our town stretched before us: the red roofs, the white-rendered buildings, the mosque minarets and church bells dotted before us. Why did anyone want to destroy something so beautiful?

I took a deep, shuddering breath. "Do you want me to read?" I asked.

"I need a laugh." Zora sat up and wiped her eyes.

I read a few paragraphs while she lay her head on my shoulder, hooking her arm around my elbow.

# 2-Hideout

Emir and I were on afternoon school shift, doing our home-work in the living room with the sound of the television in the background, when the front door burst open. Babo entered, his face pale. "Esma, Esma!"

Mama came from the kitchen. "What is it, Fadil?"

"The bus pulled up at the hotel, but Serbs surrounded it. They were wearing camouflage, holding automatic rifles, ready for war. They said they wouldn't agree to power sharing. That if we wanted Srebrenica spared, then we were to surren-der our weapons by eight tomorrow."

"What are we going to do, Fadil? We need to leave," Mama said in a panicked voice, her hands in her dark hair as if she was going to pull her hair out by the roots.

"I have to return to the hotel. We are voting on whether we're going to agree to the ultimatum or not. You and the children stay here until I return."

I tried to read my father's face. Was that fear or despair? The mask quickly came down, and he looked resolute.

I peered through the window. He walked to Zora's house. He and Slobodan conferred for a few minutes. Slobodan cov-ered his face in despair as my father left.

Mama paced around the house, lost. "I have to call my parents." Mama picked up the phone and pressed the buttons, banging the headset in the cradle. "It's dead."

"What are we going to do?" I asked. My father's fear making me tremble. Were we going to war?

"There's nothing to do but wait," Mama said.

I attempted to work on my homework again, but distractions kept me from focusing. Emir and I packed up a little while later. I went to my bedroom, signalling Zora through my bedroom window with flicking a flashlight on and off into her bedroom, which was opposite. She appeared and waved. We met outside in my backyard. I told her what my father said in a hushed whisper.

"What do you think will happen?" I asked her.

She looked at me with blue eyes wide with fear.

"What does it mean if they vote yes to the ultimatum, and we all have to surrender our weapons?" I asked, attempting to untangle this conundrum in my head.

Zora said nothing. She took my hand in hers, holding tight. Her presence calmed me. We sat quietly by the back fence, watching the trees on the hill a few metres before us. So many questions were swirling through my head about what would happen, but I was too scared to ask. Supposedly, we were now at war. After all, she was Serb; I was Bosnian. I looked at her. I could never think of Zora as my enemy. She was my best friend, the other half of me.

We parted ways half an hour later. I tried remaining awake, waiting for my father to return home to tell me what was happening, but drifted off.

A tremendous bang shook the bed. I woke up confused. Emir ran into my bedroom in his t-shirt and boxer shorts. "Get up. Get up." He yanked me by the arm from the bed, leading me down the stairs, my parents behind us.

"What's happening?" I screamed as another explosion hit the house.

"The Serbs have opened fire," Emir shouted.

We ran to the basement for shelter. Emir turned on the light. The weak bulb lit the middle of the room, the corners of the basement dark and sinister. Shelves lined the walls, jammed with boxes and camping gear. I never came down to the basement at night because the shadows made it look like a monster was hiding in its depths, but now I felt a much greater fear. The shells whistled and exploded, one on top of the other. They launched the shells in an unrelenting stream, hitting the ground with the frequency of raindrops.

I huddled against my mother's gossamer-thin white night-gown, trying to drown out the whistling of the mortar shells flying overhead. An explosion rocked the foundation of the house. Glass shattered upstairs. Dust drifted from the con-crete ceiling like snow, making me feel the house was slowly crumbling and we would suffocate under its powder.

I shivered in the cold basement. We were all barefoot, the cold of the concrete seeping into my bones. "I'm going upstairs," Babo muttered after an hour while we all huddled together, goose pimples on my skin. My teeth were chattering. He was in his pyjamas, his dark hair spiky and sticking up from the Brylcream he used to smooth his hair down.

"No, Fadil, don't." Mama tried to hold him back.

"I'll be fine." Babo squeezed her hand between his. "I need to get us clothes and coats."

He climbed up the stairs. He was gone for what seemed like forever. Finally, he returned. In his arms, he was carrying a bundle. I put my shoes on with relief, yanking the coat around me. Emir put on Babo's long coat, which only reached his knees as he was already much taller than our father.

The shelling lasted all night. Babo made us a nest in the corner, placing rubber mats and old blankets to sit on from our camping gear. We huddled, listening to the manmade thunder overhead. The earth shook, my ears rang, my eyes swam. I closed my eyes, drifting between sleep and wakefulness where everything seemed slightly unreal, my muscles moving toward the paralysis of sleep, but my eyes flinched open each time a shell landed.

Babo rummaged through the shelves opposite us.

"What are you doing, Fadil?" Mama asked tiredly.

"I hid a carton of cigarettes here." Babo moved around jars of preserves. "Got it!" he said, grabbing a box from the shelves. "Now the matches. I put candles and matches in this drawer." He rifled through a drawer next to his woodworking bench. A shell exploded above us. A jar fell from the shelf and broke next to his feet.

"For God's sake, Fadil. Leave it alone and come here," Mama exclaimed.

Babo hunted through the drawer. He finally found matches and slammed it shut. He returned to our corner and tore open the carton, his hands shaking. A shard of glass cut through his pyjamas, and he was bleeding on his calf. He shook his head, warning me not to say anything. He took out a cigarette and lit up, inhaling deeply, his whole posture relaxing.

"Give me one." Mama held out her hand. Babo held up the end of his lit cigarette and touched it at the end she was holding. I watched in surprise. Mama usually only smoked a cigarette when my parents drank their morning coffee.

Dawn broke, light spilling through the narrow windows between the ground and the foundation of the house. Dozens of half-smoked butts lay wasted on the concrete.

My stomach grumbled loudly. "I'm hungry. Aren't you?" I asked Mama.

Mama shook her head. "These kill the appetite." She held up a cigarette.

"I'll get food and water. I'll be careful," Emir said, forestalling Mama's objections.

He returned carrying bread and cheese, a bottle of water. "The Serbs have set up their artillery on the peaks ringing the town. From their position, they have a clear view down into the valley where our houses are lined up. We're like plastic figurines on a Monopoly board, ready for invasion." Emir said. "I also saw smoke curling into the air from outside our kitchen window. I think they're setting houses on fire."

Babo's brow furrowed. Mama fiddled with the cigarette butt in her hand. Srebrenica's geography was working against us. Mountains enclosed us, with only one road in and out, while the enemy encircled us and could invade at any time.

*Bang.* The front door above us slammed open. "Fadil, Esma." Slobodan appeared on the stairs. "Come with me."

"What's happening?" Babo asked.

"They're going to invade soon," Slobodan said. "Come to our house where you'll be safe."

Mama and Babo quickly exchanged glances. To the attacking Serbs, we were the enemy. We followed Slobodan to their house and into their basement. They used half of it for storage, while the other half served as a second living room for Zora's teenage brothers, with two old couches and a coffee table.

"Sit here," Zora's mother, Petra, patted the couch next to her. Zora got her ash-blonde hair and blue eyes from Petra. Mama sat, and Petra handed her the cigarette from her mouth, lighting herself another.

Slobodan and my father sat on the couch opposite, smoking too. Every time a shell crashed, they looked up at the ceiling, checking to see if it was cracking above us.

I joined Zora on the floor on top of doonas and blankets. I curled up against Zora. One of her little sisters was next to her, while another curled up against my side. Emir sat with her brothers. As the shelling continued around us, we flinched, hugging each other tight. I wondered if her parents were regretting not leaving town before the shelling started. If I'd had a choice, I would have left earlier.

In the morning, the shelling stopped, and Zora's family went upstairs. Slobodan told us we should remain out of sight in the basement. Arkan Tigers were within Srebrenica. My heart sped up as I imagined them finding us in the basement, their faces hidden by ski masks, pointing their semiautomatic weapons at us while they tortured and maimed.

I napped during the night, feeling exhausted and sore from the terror overnight. Petra and Zora brought us lunch. They told us that we were invaded, and there were soldiers patrolling the streets.

When night fell, Slobodan and his sons brought our television, cassette player, and washing machine from home. They told us that houses were being looted and appliances removed. I was relieved to have a television to distract us. My father plugged it in, turning the volume low. He flicked through the channels. They were all from Serbia, proclaiming that they were winning the war to make a Great Serbia.

Zora and Petra brought our suitcases packed with our clothes, photo albums, and jewellery. I opened my suitcase. Zora packed my diary and my favourite clothes. I followed Zora upstairs to wash in the bathroom, changing into clean clothes. The rest of my family followed suit.

Over the next few days, we settled into a routine. Slobodan and his family brought us food and news from the outside world. We only went upstairs during the night when all the curtains were down.

On the third day, Slobodan ran into the basement in a panic. "They're searching all Serb homes. They know some families are hiding our neighbours, and they're taking them away."

"What do we do?" my father asked.

"Wait until nightfall. You'll have to go to the woods." Slobodan went to the storage side of the garage, removing his tent from one shelf. My father joined him in collecting camping supplies.

My mother and Petra went upstairs to the kitchen, packing flour and vegetables in bags for us to transport. Afterwards, we stayed in the basement waiting for dark, tense and shivering with dread. When nightfall came, the shelling stopped. I kept expecting a bang on the door with Serb soldiers demanding to search the house to find us.

"It's time." Slobodan came down and helped Babo carry the tent. We went through the back door, heading towards the woods. Zora and her siblings remained behind. Slobodan was worried too many people would attract attention. We took turns running across the flat stretch to the hill one at a time. We were meeting at Ćelo. If we didn't all arrive within an hour, then we were to assume Serbs had intercepted someone. My stomach lurched, and nausea hit when my parents discussed this possibility.

My brother Emir went first. He was carrying the wooden stove on his back and ran in long strides, reaching the hill quickly.

I turned to Zora and hugged her. "I'll never forget you," I whispered in her ear.

"I'll be right here when you come back," Zora whispered. "We'll go to Ćelo together and read romance novels and giggle like usual."

"Yes, we will," I said, I struggling to believe her.

"Go Seka." My father pushed me, and I ran. I was wearing all my clothes, the layers making me bulky and thick. Mama told us to wear our clothes so our backpacks could fit essentials. My heart was hammering, each crunch of my feet amplified until I was certain the Serbs could hear me from their camps, each snap of a twig the crack of a gun. The backpack filled with food and blankets was bulky, bouncing hard against my back. I slowed as I reached the hill. It was steep and dark. The moon peeked between the clouds, lighting the way, and then disappearing again. I was thankful I climbed this trek every day for most of my adolescence. While my heart raced with panic, I ran with fleet-footed and sure steps.

"Seka," Emir whispered. He was standing under Ćelo with the wooden stove beside him. We hugged quickly. I stood quietly under Ćelo's large protective branches and waited. Mama was going to be next. I heard her before I saw her. She was crashing through the forest like a panicked animal, letting out little panting moans.

"I'm going to help her," Emir said.

I heard the patter of his footsteps and then a high-pitched shriek. He must have startled Mama. Soon after, they both joined me. Mama was huffing and puffing as she walked toward Ćelo while Emir carried her backpack.

My father and Slobodan arrived twenty minutes later. They were carrying the tent between them.

"I can help you further," Slobodan said.

"No, it won't be safe for you," Babo said. We were going to join the other Muslims hiding out in the forest. They hugged, my father holding Slobodan by the back of the head as they pressed their foreheads against each other. "Goodbye, my brother," he whispered.

"Goodbye," Slobodan said, his voice breaking. He turned and vanished into the darkness back down the mountain.

"Let's go," Babo said. "We're going to be walking most of the night."

I put on my backpack, stepping in behind my mother, while Emir went to the rear. He clipped my heels as we walked until he learnt to shorten his strides. The handles of the backpack were chafing against my shoulders from the weight, and my legs were hurting.

"Stop, intruder," a guttural male voice shouted from the darkness.

"It's Fadil Torlak," my father called out.

"*Salam Aleikum*," my mother said, the Arabic phrase of peace be upon you.

"*Aleikumu Salam*," a man said, emerging from his hiding place behind a trunk.

After greeting us, the men led us further up the mountain to an encampment. A few curious faces peered from tents or lifted their heads from their beds on the ground, a make-shift lean-to of tarpaulin and branches sheltering them. Some men my father knew helped him, and Emir set up the tent while I helped Mama arrange our belongings. Dawn lit up the sky, and I looked around. The woodlands were full of people, some in tents, while others brought tarpaulins and set up makeshift shelters. It looked like the gypsy encampments I saw when we visited my grandparents in the country. The gypsies travelled with horse and cart, following the local fair, where they gained work and could operate stalls. I always thought it would be fun to travel across the countryside, living wherever you wanted, but now that I was in the great outdoors myself, it didn't seem so romantic.

When the tent was erected, I gratefully crawled in and lay down to sleep.

I woke to a green tarpaulin flapping as leaves rustled in the breeze, a cuckoo echoing through the forest. Emir kept me warm by pressing against my side and putting his arm over me. During the night, he'd hogged the covers when he turned away from me, leaving me uncovered in the crisp night air, until I elbowed him, and he got the hint and leaned into me.

This was the closest we were in years. Once puberty hit, our casual hugs and wrestling matches stopped, but here in the forest I gained comfort from his warm body.

I sat up on the thick doona we'd used as a bed. My mother was stacking wood on the ashes of the fire that burnt out during the night. She struck a match and lit the kindling, gently blowing on it to get it going, the red glow emphasising the dark circles beneath her eyes.

I threw off the covers. I was wearing my clothes from the night before. It was April, and even though the snow had melted, the nights were chilly. My parents told me to dress in layers, so I wore my tracksuit pants over my jeans and walked stiffly.

I looked in the pot and didn't recognise the dish as anything my mother made before. She'd improvised and cut up all sorts of root vegetables, tossing in a hunk of dried meat for flavour. Emir crawled out after me and sat on a log, looking droopy-eyed.

"Maybe you and Emir can go cut up some wood for us?" Mama said to my father.

"Absolutely." Emir grabbed the axe, flexing his muscles while he used it as a barbell. "Let's go, Babo."

Babo hesitated for a moment before carefully putting out his cigarette and following him.

While they were gone, I attempted finding someone my age to spend time together, but most of them were older siblings who supervised their younger siblings. Babo and Emir returned, and my brother stacked the wood they cut into a neat pile beside the fire.

Over the next few days, the grove filled with more and more people, the camp stretching further into the forest. Some remained in their homes until the shells hit ever closer. Their Serb neighbours hid some, choosing to leave when it was no longer safe.

At night, my mother crept with other women to nearby houses to cook, raiding the kitchens of empty houses for food. The first few nights we went to the houses to bathe, but soon it became too dangerous to linger because of Serbs patrolling the streets. Then the Serbs destroyed the town's water supplies. We hiked two kilometres to the river to bathe in freezing water. Mama washed our clothes, leaving them out on rocks and branches to dry. I survived my first poo in the wilderness, digging a hole and squatting over it, using leaves to wipe myself afterwards. The thrill of the adventure had well and truly worn off.

I kept hearing one name mentioned over and over. Naser Orić, a police officer with the foresight to stockpile weapons when the conflict was nothing more than talk, was organising a rebellion. Naser was planning an attack on a convoy of Serb cars going from Srebrenica to Bratunac. In the convoy was the newly appointed nationalist Serb mayor of Srebrenica.

In the morning, I woke up to people shouting and opened my eyes in fear. Were the Serbs attacking? Babo and Mama were standing beside the fire with wide smiles on their faces.

"We can go home," Mama told me, her face glowing with relief and happiness. "Naser Orić chased them away."

The ambush was a success. The ambush resulted in the killing of twenty-eight Serbs, with no Muslim casualties. As Naser and his soldiers returned to the town, the remaining

Serbs in Srebrenica fled in panic. Later that day, we cautiously descended from the forest back into our house to find smashed glass from the broken windows sparkling on the floor and our appliances gone.

I ran to Zora's house, banging on the back door. When no one responded, I turned open the doorknob and called Zora's name. Silence echoed back. I walked in, climbing the stairs, when I heard a shuffle above. I peered above the stairs. Slobodan appeared with a rifle in his arms, pointing it directly at me.

I gasped. Was Slobodan going to shoot me?

"Seka," he said, with relief, pointing his rifle to the ground.

I heard footsteps behind me as my father climbed the stairs ahead of me. Slobodan placed the rifle against the wall and stepped down. He and my father hugged tightly. Zora peered out from behind him. I ran up the stairs and hugged her tightly.

"You're still here," Babo was saying to Slobodan.

"This is my home. I'm not leaving," Slobodan said.

Later that day, Zora's brothers helped us return the appliances from their basement to our house while Mama and I cleaned the glass. Zora's mother brought dinner, spinach and cheese pita. As we sat and ate at our dining table, it was easy to forget what was happening outside the walls of our house.

# 3-Cleansed

Zora and I were in my bedroom, lying on the bed lazily, each of us reading. We could only read during the bright light of the day because Serbs had cut off the electricity. The day it happened, Babo took our small wooden stove out into the backyard to cook all the leftover meat we had, our families eating until my stomach was sore and I felt like I was in a meat coma. Since then, we used candles, which only lasted a few days, and then Babo used an old camp oil lamp.

A shell exploded, and I fell off my bed. Zora was still sitting on the bed; I grabbed her arm, yanking her down. The shells were close, making the house shake and rumble like we were in an earthquake. "We need to go to the basement," I said.

We stood. Zora peered out the window at her house. "Noooo," she screamed.

I looked too, freezing for a split second. A shell landed on the roof of her house, splitting it open, leaving a gaping hole.

"Let's go." I half-carried her to the door, and we ran down the stairs. Mama and Emir were waiting in the hallway.

Zora headed for the front door. "I have to see my family."

I hesitated, eyeing the basement door.

Babo appeared from the kitchen. "Go to the basement. I'll check on your family."

I yanked Zora, following my mother and brother downstairs. The shelling was unrelenting every second, one after another. I hugged Zora close as dust fell from the ceiling. She was tense, staring at the stairs, willing her family to arrive.

I heard thudding footsteps above us; Babo appeared, Slobodan's arm around his neck as he helped him to walk. Slobodan was bleeding from the head and looked dazed. Behind them were Petra and Zora's siblings. Zora ran to her mother, hugging her tight. I breathed a sigh of relief to see they were safe. Petra recounted that when the roof collapsed, Slobodan got struck by a beam.

Babo helped Slobodan sit and searched the shelves for a cloth. He found an old shirt, tearing it into strips, then holding it against Slobodan's temple to stem the wound. Slobodan's eyes closed.

"No, no," Mama said, gently shaking him. "You can't sleep."

As the shells thundered, I huddled against the basement wall with Zora and our siblings while the adults conferred about whether to take Slobodan to the hospital. They decided it was too dangerous. Mama monitored Slobodan, waking him every hour, asking him questions to check his cognition, and holding up his fingers to check his vision.

The shelling continued until night came. Slobodan insisted on seeing his house. I followed Zora up the stairs. Shells pockmarked her house. A gaping hole in the roof was caused by the front wall of the house caving in.

Petra fell to her knees, crying as her children huddled around her, shocked and teary-eyed.

"Slobodan Đokić," a man shouted through a megaphone from the hills above us. "Traitors of Greater Serbia will be punished." He then used many profanities, swearing at Slobodan, threatening his family.

"Let's get away from here," Mama urged, helping Petra stand and taking her back into our house. "We'll evaluate the damage in the morning."

In our house we couldn't hear the megaphone as clearly, but the voice droned on for an hour, different soldiers taking turns swearing and threatening Zora's family and other Serbs who remained, their voices slurred and gruff. Babo said they were blustering on alcohol fumes.

I hugged Zora tightly against me, pushing her ear against my chest, covering her other ear so she couldn't hear it. Mama collected blankets and pillows that she used to make beds for Zora's family in our living room, using our camping supplies.

I didn't want to leave Zora alone; she didn't want to leave her family, so I slept curled up against her. Petra lay next to Slobodan and woke him every hour, following my mother's protocol.

In the morning, we walked with Zora's family to their house. It looked even worse in the bright light of day. Her couch was halfway out of the house, the display cabinets her mother used for crockery exploded, with shards of ceramics littering the inside and outside of the house.

Slobodan and my father went inside carefully, checking the structure of the house. They spent the day laboriously excavating the rubble for personal effects and belongings. The back of the house, where the kitchen and spare room faced away from the mountains, was intact. Slobodan and Petra shifted the belongings that were undamaged: one sofa, one armchair, a table and two chairs, into the one room.

Babo offered for them to live with us, but Slobodan wouldn't abandon his house. He said he would repair it as soon as he could. We spent the day helping them arrange their quarters to sleep in.

Our house sustained damage too, a hole in the roof and shattered windows. Babo went to town and returned with plastic sheets that we nailed over the windows; we boarded up the windows that faced the mountain where the enemy was, including my bedroom. Babo climbed a ladder to fix the roof tiles.

"Don't be foolish, Fadil," Mama shouted. "A sniper will shoot you."

"The soldiers are sleeping off their night drinking," Babo said calmly as he methodically repaired the broken tiles on our roof.

Babo just climbed down the ladder when a shell exploded in our front yard. We ran to the basement, and Zora's family joined us.

We spent another day huddled in the basement's darkness. When we came up again Zora's house was no more. Shells decimated it, including the two rooms that were their refuge. Our house sustained more damage, too, but Babo was confident he could repair it.

"You can live with us," Babo said, hugging Slobodan.

"No," Slobodan shook his head. "Then you will be a target. We need to go further away."

Slobodan and Petra moved into Boris's house, which was only a few streets away from us. I helped her carry her belongings; even though we were only a 10-minute walk away from each other, it still felt like the ending of something. We had grown up being next to each other, seeing each other without effort. Now we would have to navigate shelling and snipers to visit. Each trip would be precarious and dangerous. I gripped her hand as her parents walked ahead of us. "I have to go," she said.

I nodded, wiping a tear and let go of her hand.

The work brigade drafted Babo. Every third night, he would report for duty and work tirelessly at a network of trenches along the front line. He chopped down trees, building earth, stone, and log bunkers. They paid him in food, and we desperately needed the rations. Slobodan tried to volunteer, but they turned him away. The soldiers on our side called him a spy, made accusations he would report to the enemy.

Babo and Slobodan sat up all night, drinking the last of the *rakija* from last summer's harvest.

"I am Srebrenician first, second and third," Slobodan raged. "And they won't let me defend my own home."

"It's these new people coming in here. They don't have the same view about who we are."

Surrounding villagers who were ethnically cleansed from their homes flooded Srebrenica, seeking refuge. Emir and I climbed up the nearby hill Kalina to see the single paved road that wound southeast from Srebrenica toward the Bosnian border town Skelani, leading across a bridge to Serbia. From the hilltop, we saw enemy patrols pass back and forth. Tendrils of white smoke rose into the sky, blooming like flowers over the graves of Bosnian Muslim villages to the southeast. Lines of villagers formed a column marching down the main road that led to Srebrenica. Men, women, and children. Some of them were carrying bags or bundles of what looked like clothing. Some of them walked with their livestock, others carried parcels of goods, while yet others were empty-handed.

Zora was visiting me when a family with a horse and cart stopped in front of her house. They climbed down, foraging in the rubble of Zora's house, talking among themselves. The wife was wearing *dimije*, harem-type pants worn only by peasant women in the villages, a headscarf covering her hair. She dug a fork out of the earth.

I ran downstairs, Zora hot on my heels, calling my mother. My father was away at the brigade. Emir was visiting a friend.

"*Merhaba*," Mama called out, stepping out of our house.

I looked at her askance. We never used Muslim salutations. The family looked up, returning her greeting of welcome.

"Those belong to our neighbours," Mama said.

"They're not here, and we are," the man said brusquely, wearing a black beret and chequered shirt.

"They had to move. They're still in Srebrenica," Mama said.

The man and woman stood. The woman threw the fork to the ground. Zora walked toward her, picking it up.

"Let's go, children," he said.

His son dug out something from the rubble, wiped the dust off it. His father looked over; it was a silver cross that Zora's mother displayed in a cabinet, an heirloom passed down from her parents.

"You're protecting Serbs," the man shouted at Mum.

Zora stepped back from his rage.

"You're protecting the scum who chased us out of our home." He stepped forward, snatching the fork from Zora.

Zora ran back to my mother's side. "She's just a child. She's not to blame for any of this." Mama pushed me and Zora behind her.

"But her parents are." The man raged and swore.

Mama ushered us into the house, bolting the door shut. We watched from the window as the family searched through the rubble for half an hour, collecting whatever valuables they could. I held Zora as she cried heart-wrenching sobs where she could barely catch her breath. After that day, she didn't want to visit. She said she didn't want to see the graveyard of her old life, so we would only see each other when I went to her.

When we visited, Babo and Slobodan drank in the living room.

"People I've known my whole life are acting like me and my family are pariahs. They don't want to be seen to be siding with us." Slobodan slammed his shot glass onto the table.

"This whole world is upside down," my father said. "It just makes little sense."

Babo forbade Emir from volunteering for the army. When Babo left for the work brigade, Emir went to the army headquarters at the post office with his rifle. Emir hunted with my uncle and grandfather in the village since he was a small boy and was an excellent shot. After the army commander tested his shooting skills in the woods, Emir passed and was accepted onto the front lines. Babo raged when he came home but to no avail. Emir saw himself as the great defender of his homeland. Unlike our father, he did not feel conflicted. To Emir it was simple: the enemy encircled us and was attempting to strangle us in their net. While our father saw shades of grey, those who were shooting us were the pawns of nationalist politicians, and if we just waited, this would pass. In the end, Babo insisted on being transferred to the front line to keep an eye on Emir.

I, too, found it hard to deal with these shades of grey, and when I was with Zora, we avoided talking about the war. Instead, we reminisced about the life we lived before. No longer could we run heedless into the forest to be idle. Now all our interactions were in a back bedroom of the house she lived in with her family that was safe from snipers and shells.

While my father and brother were at the front, I slept with my mother in my parent's bed in case the shelling started. Mama restlessly twisted and turned beside me. She worried about my father, but it was Emir who was her heart, and the thought of his loss weighed on her. During the day she paced up and down the house, lifting the phone and checking to see if she could call my grandparents.

Since the phone lines were down, she hadn't been able to call her family. We'd listened to the news, but for weeks the enemy controlled the local airwaves and broadcast repeated appeals for all Serbs everywhere to join the fight for a Greater Serbia. According to these broadcasts, the Muslims started the war. The Muslims were the aggressors, with no mention it was the Serbs who ended the delegation and handed out ultimatums.

Mama visited the box office at the Cultural Centre every day, which served as the reception point for newly arrived refugees, where officials registered them and assigned them a place to live. At first, they would receive either an empty apartment or house left by Serbs or Bosnians, but as refugees kept arriving, officials assigned them to public buildings. Mama learned from the refugees that the enemy's troops, who invaded and were later expelled, had looted and ransacked most of the deserted houses, leaving behind no household appliances. Then hungry Bosniak refugees looted the houses again. Every day, she looked more and more listless and drawn as she didn't find her parents' names on the lists of arriving refugees.

I found her in her bedroom, browsing through her photo albums. As I approached, she gently caressed her parent's faces.

"I think they're gone," she whispered, her voice hopeless.

"We don't know that. They could still be on their way." I sat on the bed next to her, placing my arm around her shoulders.

"I'm so scared." Mama lay her head on my shoulder. "Every day that your brother and father are gone, I'm scared they won't return. They'll vanish like my parents have."

I held her tightly, tears seeping down my face as I comforted her. My mother was so strong and stoic, yet she was breaking under the strain. All I could do was hold her and pray to a God I wasn't sure was listening.

As refugees arrived from the surrounding villages, they harassed Zora and her family. One night, a Muslim family attempted to evict them forcibly from the house through a blaze of fisticuffs and brutal violence. The next day when I visited with my father, Zora's brothers and father had bruised faces. They only prevailed when her older brother produced a hunting rifle that was left behind. Thankfully, the Muslim villagers didn't test their will. The rifle had no ammunition.

Babo helped them barricade all the doors and windows by nailing planks of wood over them. Zora's parents could only leave the house one at a time. Her brothers and father took turns being on guard, watching through barricaded windows for desperate refugees who wanted to try their luck again.

When I next visited Zora, I discovered that the house they were staying in had been shelled throughout the night. Only the back of the house remained after the shelling destroyed the front.

"My father thinks that they're targeting us again. He says someone has betrayed us and told the enemy where we are."

I wanted to comfort Zora, tell her it wasn't true, but I knew better.

"He's making plans for us to leave."

My breath expelled in a rush, as if someone punched me in the stomach. I wanted to beg Zora to stay, to not leave, but as I looked at her face, the words stilled on my tongue. She was wan and drawn, her eyes were red with dark circles beneath them.

Being surrounded by the enemy shelling us made it hard enough, but she and her family faced double persecution. To those in Srebrenica, they were the enemy, even though they were not the aggressors, and to the enemy, they were traitors.

"My parents want us to have a fresh start. Somewhere where it won't matter who or what we are. They want us to go to Australia."

"Wow, Australia is great." I wiped my eyes. My uncle Mustafa, my mother's brother, lived in Australia. We visited him once when I was ten years old and stayed for a month. When we left Bosnia, snow blanketed the ground and when we arrived in Australia, the heat of summer was so fierce it burnt my skin raw on the first day; I spent the next four weeks peeling and sore.

"Maybe one day you'll come visit." Zora clasped my hand. She was crying too.

"Sure."

Australia was so far away it took a whole 24 hours to travel by aeroplane. My uncle only returned once in the twenty years since he migrated, and the only reason we visited was because my father attended a conference. I wanted Zora to be safe, but I also knew that once she left, chances were we would never see each other again.

# 4. Escape

I walked to town holding Zora's hand. My father heard convoys were leaving Srebrenica. We walked to the department store to find crowds gathered around the huge aid trucks that towered as large as the department store roof. The trays were now full of women, a few with bundles of belongings they placed at their feet, their arms free to hold their children.

Babo approached one of the Bosnian soldiers standing guard, wearing a camouflage t-shirt and black jeans because our side didn't have enough uniforms or weapons, the rifle over his chest the only indicator he was a soldier. "Only women and children. They won't be able to leave." He pointed at Emir and Zora's two brothers, aged 16 and 17, who looked like grown adults with their hairy cheeks and towering height.

Slobodan's face dropped in despair. Only Zora and her two younger sisters would be getting out. "Petra, you'll have to go with the children."

Zora's mother began crying, her pale skin flushing, as she hugged her two younger daughters tightly against her side. "I'm not leaving any of my children behind."

Hearing Zora's mother's name, Camouflage T-shirt looked closer at Slobodan. "What is your name?" he asked.

Slobodan told him his name. Camouflage T-Shirt tightened his hands on the rifle. "You will not take the place of one of our own." He lifted the rifle, pointing it at Slobodan.

I gasped, holding Zora tighter against me as we backed away from the crazed soldier. Why was he reacting like this? We were all one people. There was no way of telling a Muslim from a Serb based on physical appearance. Slobodan and my father were both dark-haired and blue-eyed. They looked like brothers. Yet this soldier was acting like Zora and her family were somehow a threat.

Babo pushed himself in front of the rifle. "Calm down. This is a good man. He just wants to leave with his family."

"He's a Serb," Camouflage T-Shirt spat out.

"We're going now," Babo said, holding up his hands as he walked backwards, forcing Slobodan to step backwards as well.

Camouflage T-Shirt hesitated. A woman screamed to the left of us; he turned his head. Desperate refugees attempted to climb onto the already full tray. A woman was on the ground, her leg bent in an unnatural direction as she screamed with pain.

Refugees milled between us and Camouflage T-Shirt, hiding us from view.

"Hurry, hurry," Babo urged, running away from the department store.

I held Zora's hand on the run home, arriving with a stitch in my side.

"What are we going to do now?" Slobodan asked as we entered our house.

My father told Mama what happened.

Zora and I climbed up my stairs, her younger siblings following us, leaving the adults to figure out a plan. I took relief in the fact that I had covered my window with plastic, ensuring that we couldn't see Zora's house. It would only cause her pain to see it as it was now.

"Do you want to play Uno?" I asked, getting out the cards.

"Sure," Zora said, her younger sisters sitting on each side of her. We played in sober silence until the doorbell rang. I came downstairs to find Mama embracing my grandparents. Sweat soaked Nana's blouse, and her swarthy face turned pale. She was dark-haired with dark-set small eyes that proclaimed she was of Ottoman Turkish heritage. Beside her was my grandfather, who I called Dido, his pale skin sunburnt. My Aunt Adna, my mother's younger sister, led Nana to the sofa and sat her down while Mama rushed into the kitchen, returning with a glass of water.

My Uncle Ibrahim was behind them, with my grandmother's darker complexion and hooded eyes. He ushered in my Aunt Paša and my three cousins. Along with them were a woman and a boy. Blonde wisps of the woman's hair poked through her headscarf. She clutched the boy, who was head and shoulders taller than her, like he was her life buoy while she drowned in the ocean. The boy had his mother's colouring—blonde hair and clear blue eyes—their pale skin translucent so that their veins were visible.

"This is Edina and her son Ramo," my uncle Ibrahim introduced them after we exchanged greetings and hugs amongst the family.

Ramo offered his hand; I was impressed that even amidst this chaotic introduction, he adhered to our schooling by the

Union of Pioneers of Yugoslavia to always offer a handshake. Ramo's callused palm scraped on my palm.

My pulse raced; it became harder to breathe. I glanced over at Zora. Her eyes were wide with curiosity as she glanced at Ramo.

"Tristan," I whispered in her ear.

She giggled. He looked like the hero in the romance novel we were reading.

"The two of you are related," Ibrahim said, looking at Ramo and me.

My stomach plunged. Oh, God, I was lusting after a cousin.

"Ramo's mother is Ramiza's sister," my uncle said.

I couldn't place Ramiza. My mother's family was so large it was hard to keep track of all my aunts and uncles and cousins. They spread all over the world with interconnections everywhere.

"Ramiza is Uncle Harun's wife. They live in Germany," Emir said. Harun was my mother's brother.

Thank God. We weren't blood relatives. We were only related by marriage. I could lust again.

Ramo offered his hand to Zora, but as my father introduced Zora's parents and her siblings, he winced as if he smelt dog shit, withdrawing his hand.

"Serbs," he said, looking at Zora's family like they were vermin.

"Slobodan is a family friend," my father said. "When we were invaded, they offered us shelter, and now we are returning the favour."

Ramo kept his hand by his side but said nothing.

My grandfather shook hands with Slobodan while my uncle Ibrahim remained on the outer edge, away from Zora's family.

"We'd better get going," Slobodan said, ushering Petra and his family to the door.

I unleashed a death stare at Ramo. I couldn't believe I lusted after him. He was so ugly. Ramo stared at me balefully.

Mama was lit with happiness. I helped her bring in chairs from the dining room to seat our family, then followed her to the kitchen.

"Fill the jug with water and serve it," Mama commanded, bustling between the fridge and the cool room built to store food.

I carried out a tray with a jug of water and glasses as instructed. Mama followed with plates of cut-up bread, cheese, and pickled goods. I handed out the glasses and poured water. My family ate ravenously, chomping on large chunks of bread.

My grandmother and Mum sat on the couch next to each other. They were almost mirror images of each other with the same dark hair and eyes, round faces and small mouths. Except that, like in the village, Nana had a black and mustard patterned headscarf tied around her head, a pink blouse with a blue woollen vest she knitted herself and *dimije*, loose pants tied with a drawstring around her waist. While Mama's dark hair was short and uncovered, and she was wearing city attire of knee length black skirt and a pink blouse.

My grandfather took off his blue beret. Babo offered him a cigarette, and my grandfather lit up gratefully. Dido usually only smoked hand-rolled cigarettes.

After they ate, Mama ushered my grandparents upstairs, my Aunt Adna following them.

"Did you bring your medication?" Mama asked as they climbed the stairs.

"We didn't have time to get anything, child," Dido said.

Nana was a diabetic and took a pill twice a day.

"That's okay. We'll go to the doctor and get medication later," Mama said, her voice worried.

"Can you find a room for Edina and Ramo?" Uncle Ibrahim asked my mother when she returned downstairs.

I looked over at Edina. She had eaten nothing and stared vacantly into space, rocking in her chair. Ramo was beside her, eating with one hand, while his mother held his other hand.

"They can take Emir's room," Mama said. "Come on."

Ramo carefully held his mother's elbow, helping her to her feet. He urged her to the stairs. "Don't worry, Mama, I'll stay with you."

I glanced away. Even though he was a caring son, he was a shitty person. I would never forgive him for the way he treated Zora.

My Aunt Paša was on the couch, rocking her youngest in her arms. My cousins, Imran and Minka, were wilting against her.

"Seka, take your aunt to your room so she can rest," Mama said.

I showed them to my room, taking out extra blankets and pillows from the linen cupboard and then helping my aunt make up a makeshift bed on the floor for my two cousins. She covered them with blankets when they lay down.

"Close the curtains, please, Seka." My aunt lay on the bed with the baby.

Downstairs, Mama and Ibrahim were sitting on the couch.

"Ibrahim, what happened?" Mama asked.

"It was the White Eagles and the Yugoslav National Army," my uncle said. The Yugoslav National Army was appropriated by the Serbs, and now they had all the might and artillery of the national army at their disposal.

"I thought we would still be all right, that our Serb neighbours would take care of us." Ibrahim took a sip of water. "The Bosniak police officers were told to hand over their weapons. Someone knocked on my door. The Eagles searched my house, overturning all the furniture, slashing our couch with a knife. With them was my neighbour. He told them I owned a hunting rifle; they demanded I surrender it. I went downstairs to the basement and handed it over. Goran demanded all my money. He climbed the stairs, pilfering Paša's jewellery and taking the gold necklace her mother gave her. We celebrated Orthodox Christmas together. *Bajram* together, and just like that, he turned on us."

"Ramo's father informed us that bloated, rotting corpses littered the river Drina. He recognised the school principal. We heard that the doctor and mayor went missing, and then someone said that they were floating down the river, their throats cut." Ibrahim shook his head. "We knew we had to get out, but Serbs blocked the roads between town and when the Serbs cut the phone lines, we knew something was coming. I kept watch during the night and saw someone in the field at the back digging up vegetables. I ran out to find an old man who left his apartment facing the bridge after seeing the Eagles cutting the throats of men, women and children then throwing them in the river. He told me he was an eyewitness, and he had to escape. I took him into the house, giving him bread and food. The last I saw, he was rushing to the woods."

Goose pimples broke out on my skin as I listened to the horror. I tried to picture the bridge in the village I crossed numerous times, now a site of violence and death, and shuddered. Death violated and erased the memories of my childhood.

Ibrahim stopped and sipped his water. "The next day, word came to go to the high school for an evacuation. We prepared what we could carry and walked down. My former classmate was at the high school. He approached when the Eagles were looking away and quietly whispered for us not to get on the bus. I asked him how could we get away? He said he couldn't say anymore that the Eagles would kill him for helping a Muslim. He yelled at another group of Muslims, 'come on *Balije*' before prodding them in the back with his rifle, while the Eagles looked on with approval."

Ibrahim stopped, remembering the image of his friend helping him, only to attack other Muslims.

"The Eagles were pushing people onto buses. I told Mama to pretend to collapse so we could return home. It wasn't hard for her to pretend. She was already so stressed being so near the Eagles who were abusing and hitting people. We said we needed to return to get her medication from home. We quickly packed up a bundle of food and water before hiding in the woods with other refugees."

"We planned on hiding until the Serbs left. The next day, we heard a crackling sound. At first we thought it was gunshots, but then we realised it was the sound of a blaze. We couldn't see the houses in our village because of the trees, but we could see a faint orange glow in the sky above it—it took a big fire to cast such a glow."

Ibrahim sighed heavily. "We took turns keeping watch throughout the night. The next day, we heard the squeal of a diving aeroplane; it grunted like a gigantic pig was flying over our heads. They shot at us from the sky with cannons. The woods exploded, with debris flying around us. The earth flew up as the cannons hit the ground."

I gasped, covering my mouth as I cried.

"We ran deeper into the woods and walked and walked. We found Edina and Ramo in one village we passed through. Before leaving the village, they took her husband and three other sons off the bus. The Serbs wouldn't let any men pass who could join the Bosnian army. They had nowhere to go, and Edina was a husk of a woman, so we took her with us."

Ibrahim rubbed his eyes tiredly. Now that the story was told, he seemed to shrivel.

"You're tired. You need to lie down." Mama took him up-stairs.

Emir and I followed our parents to their bedroom. Mama made us up a bed on the floor from a sponge mattress and a doona. A heaviness pressed on my chest. I floated above my grandparent's village of Kobilja Glava behind my closed eyes. The hamlet where my grandparents lived was a village of about 15 houses dotted along an unsealed, narrow dirt road. Their house was a small white rendered with a red roof. Behind it was a fenced-off area with a henhouse where the chickens squawked and a barn for the cows.

We visited every summer, and I spent the long, hot days running with the village children, climbing fruit trees and picking dark, shiny plums and sweet red cherries that we'd eat until our stomachs hurt. I'd spend hours with my grandmother watching foreign movies on the television, reading her the subtitles as she couldn't read herself, breathing in her scent: a faint tinge of hay for she tended to the cows first thing in the morning and menthol from the muscle cream she used to ease the pain of arthritis in her knees. My grandfather would come in to drink coffee, rolling up his own cigarettes and blowing smoke toward the ceiling.

I couldn't believe that the house that my mother was born in, where my grandmother had birthed all twelve of her children, was gone. The village that was the fabric of my life belonged to the Serbs. While I saw enough death and violence to know that we were all at risk, I'd still had a veneer of denial. This happened to others, not to us.

Now I knew how precarious our hold on our home was. The Serbs could burst through at any time, and we would be rootless, like Zora and her family.

The hushed silence of the house surrounded me as if it accepted its new inhabitants into its heart and hearth. Eventually, fatigue dragged me down.

The next day, my father and I walked to Zora's house straight after breakfast. Zora and I sat outside in the garden while our fathers made a plan for their escape from Srebrenica.

"We're leaving tonight," Zora said. "My father says we have to sneak over into Serb territory and pretend that we have been on the run since Srebrenica was invaded," Zora said.

I nodded, remembering the threats and epithets that the enemy in the mountains shouted at her father. If Zora and her family walked into their arms, they would not be safe. Their only chance was to contact soldiers who might not know them.

We spent the day reminiscing about our childhood, a pall of sadness hanging over us. I didn't want to go home; Babo felt the same. This was our last chance to be with our friends.

"I wish I could write to you," I told Zora.

"Me too." Zora held my hand tighter. "We've spent every day of our lives next door to each other. I can't stand the thought of not knowing what happens to you after I leave."

We were supposed to be epic lifelong friends.

"What if we write to each other in a notebook, and when this war is over, we find each other? Then we can read about everything that happened after today."

"Yes, that's it." Zora kissed my hand. "We have to promise that we'll write every day and that one day, we'll find each other in Australia."

I nodded, tears falling down my cheeks. "I'll come and find you in Australia."

We spent the afternoon scavenging for a notebook and pencil each in Boris' house.

"We need to carry it with us always so that way we can write at any time, and it doesn't get left behind if we have to leave suddenly," Zora said. She knew too well the loss of your whole life in a moment.

We found an old sheet that we cut up into a parcel to wrap the notebooks in, sewing on a long belt so we could tie our notebooks to our waist.

"How does it look?" Zora lifted her arms and twirled.

"I can't see it under your loose t-shirt," I said.

"Good." Zora nodded. "What about you?"

"I think you tied it too tightly." Zora loosened the knot, and I re-tied it, ensuring it wasn't cutting into my skin. "Perfect."

When night came, Zora and her family prepared their belongings. Babo and Slobodan pored over a map, preparing a route that would take Zora and her family away from Bosnian-held territory into Serbia.

I insisted on walking with her to Ćelo. My father tried to talk me out of it, but in the end, he agreed. It was a full moon, and the side of the mountain was lit up. We walked without talking so we didn't attract the attention of the Serbs on the mountain looking for an easy target.

Zora and I stood under Ćelo. I gave Zora the goodbye gift I prepared, an identical necklace to match mine. Emir gave me his coin that he'd bored a hole into so I could thread a chain through. "Now, no matter where you are in the world, we will be connected forever," I whispered in Zora's ear as I hugged her.

She lifted her hand and held the surface of the coin, caressing President Tito's profile as tears streamed down her face. "I love you, Seka." She kissed me on the cheek. She joined her family, and they disappeared into the darkness.

My father held me tightly against him as I cried.

We trudged back down the mountain and to our house. I wondered whether Zora and her family would make it through to safety. Would I ever know if they were alright? With every step she took out of Srebrenica, she was one step away from me and into an unknown future. The darkness spread from the night into my heart.

Within a few days, our household settled into a routine of sorts. My cousins wanted to play hide and seek, but we couldn't go outside, and there were only so many hiding places in the house. We regularly took shelter from shelling in the basement when we feared the roof would collapse on us.

Ramo's mother was struggling. Overwhelmed by grief, she remained in the attic, prostrate on the bed we set up for her, staring at the wall behind her. Today, Mama cajoled her downstairs and into the living room, where they were partaking in their daily ritual of drinking coffee. The coffee beans were scarce, so Mama started making the coffee weak.

Before the war she used to heap six teaspoons into the *džezva*, coffee pot, boiling it over the stove until it was a frothing and bubbling, a glossy mess of black gold. Mama boiled the milk until thick bits of cream floated on top—my parents drank coffee first thing in the morning, before eating breakfast, and at night. Now, there was no milk or sugar, so the coffee became coloured water, but still, all the grown-ups gathered for their daily ritual.

My brother and father returned from the front the day before, uninjured but exhausted and filthy. While they were drinking coffee, my Uncle Ibrahim asked about the Chetniks, which was the name of the Serb nationalist movement those from the villages used in World War II.

"They're not as hungry as we are. The international community imposed sanctions, but the Vojvodina is big and fertile, and the Serbs will never go hungry." Babo took a tiny sip of his watered-down coffee, closing his eyes in pleasure as the warmth worked its way down his body.

"They're only two hundred metres away." Emir gulped his coffee, unable to savour it. "I watch them through my binoculars, and they watch us back. We don't shoot. We don't have the ammunition to spare."

"They just have to wait us out. Hunger is their most effective weapon." Dido took a drag, blowing smoke out of his nostrils.

Imran climbed into my uncle's lap, and Minka climbed into my aunt's lap. The baby was asleep on the floor beside my aunt.

"If they knew the truth, that I only had five bullets in my shotgun, we'd be dead," Babo said.

"Thankfully, Naser Orić keeps them on their toes by fighting guerrilla warfare like the Partisans did in WWII," Emir continued. Naser was the Bosnian Army Commander. "We fight like the Partisans, either to win or retreat despite being outgunned and outmatched. We fight and take as much of their ammunition as we can, then rest and go again before they can prepare a defence. If we didn't have Naser, we'd be dead." Emir spoke of Naser with reverence in his voice.

"Naser is not a God. He's a 25-year-old who has some military training," Babo said sharply.

I slowly edged to the back of the living room. As the argument began between the adults about the best way of dealing with the war, I quietly snuck up the stairs to my parents' bedroom, then onto their balcony for some peace and quiet. I ducked to avoid attracting snipers or shells. When Mama saw me on the balcony the first time, she nearly had a conniption and demanded that I leave, so I learnt to exit through the glass doors then re-arrange the curtains behind me so no one could tell I was outside.

I took my notebook out of the pouch around my waist.

*"Every day without you is one of sadness and boredom. I forget you're gone and try to go to your house, and each time I'm grief-stricken when I see it demolished and gone."*

I dutifully wrote to Zora every day. At first my letters were long, full of the mundane details of survival, but then became short daily updates as boredom at my plight set in.

I was sitting on the concrete floor when I heard wood clanking. I leaned over and peered at the roof. The attic window was open, and Ramo peered through. I sat back on the balcony so he wouldn't see me.

He attempted to engage me in a conversation during our first meal together. He only bothered me once. I would not be friendly with a xenophobe. We now carefully avoided each other. This should have been difficult in a house that had eight adults, three adolescents, and three children, yet somehow it was easy. We always sat on opposite sides of the group during meals and while I could hear his conversation with my brother sometimes, we never spoke to each other.

*"I haven't forgiven Ramo for the way he treated you and refuse to speak to him. I hope you've made it to safety and will be in Australia soon."*

She and her family hopefully made it to the Serb territory and were being transported to a town that cared for refugees. Her father said they would apply for a refugee visa to Australia as soon as he could, but these things took months. I drowsily closed my eyes on the balcony and played out my favourite fantasy, where my family, too, left Srebrenica.

We went to Australia—I filled in the details from my hazy memories years before of bright blue skies, biting sun, and flat suburban streets that stretched to the horizon. Zora and I found each other. The details were hazy. I was walking down the street, and I spotted a blonde-haired girl walking ahead of me in a huddle with other girls who were shorter than her. Her long stride and lithe form were familiar in a flowing bright red dress, the breeze moulding it around her. The girl laughed at something one girl she was with said. Her head turned, and I saw that familiar profile I had traced with my eyes most of my life: the snub nose, high top lip, delicately pink nostrils on a pale face. "Zora," I called.

She stopped and turned, her face puzzled as she looked me over. In my fantasy, I was wearing tight jeans and a white Nike t-shirt, the denim clinging to my curves while the t-shirt moulded to my chest. My hair was long, reaching my waist, the curls large and wind-blown, tasteful makeup on my face. Zora smiled with delight as she recognised me. She ran toward me, leaving the girls behind. I ran toward her and suddenly we were in each other's arms, and it was like home.

"I found you," I whispered against her ear as I breathed in her scent of roses.

"I can't believe it," she said, tears dripping down her face.

I opened my eyes and wiped the tears on my cheek. It was a bright blue sky, like the one in my fantasy, but nothing before me resembled my dream of freedom. I gazed over the balcony at the rubble that was Zora's house, my heart aching as reality ripped away the last moments of joy.

I returned the notebook and crawled back into the house, standing up when I was behind the curtain and was unseen by any potential snipers.

# Contextualising the Breakup of Yugoslavia

When I began writing *The Tree That Stood Still*, I knew that I had to first make sense of the political earthquake that shattered the country of my ancestry—Yugoslavia. The novel opens in Srebrenica in 1992, a town where Muslims, Serbs, and Croats once lived as neighbours, colleagues, and even family. My protagonist, Seka Torlak, and her best friend Zora, a Serb, are fictional, but they represent very real relationships and communities that were torn apart when Yugoslavia fractured under the weight of nationalism and war.

Telling this story required me to reach back to the early 1980s, when Josip Broz Tito's death marked the beginning of Yugoslavia's decline. Under Tito's rule, ethnic tensions were suppressed under the ideology of "brotherhood and unity." My parents were raised in this system, taught to identify as Yugoslavs first, to celebrate shared holidays, and to marry across ethnic lines. But after Tito, old grievances resurfaced, and nationalism began to seep into public discourse like poison.

By the early 1990s, Slovenia and Croatia had declared independence. Bosnia and Herzegovina followed after a referendum in 1992, despite opposition from many Bosnian Serbs. What unfolded next was not just war—it was a project of ethnic cleansing. In the novel, I show this through the lives of ordinary people: the neighbours who stop speaking, the schoolmates who vanish, the families who flee in the dead of night. These aren't just background details—they are the threads of my own family history, of stories whispered between relatives and recounted in news bulletins that were watched in tears.

In writing Seka's story, I wanted to explore how the national unraveling felt at street level. I used fiction to distill the fear, the confusion, and the betrayal that so many experienced. In one chapter, Seka watches her classroom empty out, noting that the missing students are all Serbs. Her best friend Zora starts to receive threatening calls at night, demanding her father take up arms. Seka is bewildered. Just weeks earlier, they were planning to attend veterinary school together. Now they are being told they belong to opposing camps.

That moment of confusion and heartbreak mirrors my own process of understanding. I was a teenager in Australia during the war. I watched it unfold on TV, read about it in headlines, and listened as my mother wept quietly over the phone with relatives. It didn't make sense to me that one day we were Yugoslav, and the next day, my Muslim background could mark me as a target. I poured all of that into Seka—the grief of a young girl trying to hold onto her identity while the world tells her she must pick a side.

Srebrenica, where much of the novel is set, was declared a UN "safe area" in 1993, yet the siege worsened. Food shortages, black markets, and sniper fire became part of daily life. I tried to show this creeping desperation: families foraging for firewood, boiling dandelions for tea, bartering for medicine. At the same time, I wanted to honour the resilience—the ways people found to carry on. Seka and Zora sew notebooks into waist pouches to write to each other after they are separated. In a world falling apart, they invent a private system of memory and hope.

The war culminated, as we know, in the 1995 genocide—when 8,372 Bosniak men and boys murdered in Srebrenica. Though my novel ends before that point, every scene is shadowed by the knowledge of what's coming. Every goodbye is fraught with finality. Every friendship is precious and fragile. When Seka and Zora part ways, they do so without knowing if they'll ever see each other again. That uncertainty haunts me because for many, including members of my extended family, it was reality.

Writing *The Tree That Stood Still* allowed me to honour the Yugoslavia I grew up hearing about—the multicultural, pluralistic dream—and to bear witness to the tragedy of its dissolution. I didn't write this book to provide political analysis. I wrote it to tell a story of loss, love, and resistance. I wanted readers, especially young adults, to feel the heartbreak of a friendship torn apart by war and to understand that history doesn't just happen in parliaments or battlefields—it happens in homes, in schools, and between friends.

In telling Seka's story, I was telling my own. Not as a survivor of the siege, but as a child of the diaspora, trying to piece together the shrapnel of memory, history, and identity. Through fiction, I could explore the emotional truths that facts alone can't reach. This novel is my attempt to ensure that what happened in Srebrenica is not forgotten.

Amra Pajalic

# Teaching resources

## CHAPTER 1

### Vocabulary Bank

| Word | Definition | Synonyms |
| --- | --- | --- |
| Stamina | The ability to sustain prolonged physical or mental effort. | |
| Commemorate | To honour the memory of a person or event. | |
| Melancholy | A feeling of deep sadness or sorrow. | |
| Nationalist | A person who strongly identifies with their nation and supports its interests. | |
| Intimidation | The act of frightening or threatening someone. | |
| Ethnic | Relating to a population subgroup with a common national or cultural tradition. | |
| Secluded | Sheltered and private; away from the public eye. | |
| Persevere | To continue in a course of action despite difficulty or lack of success. | |
| Propaganda | Information, especially biased or misleading, used to promote a cause. | |

## Comprehension Questions

1. Who is the main character of the story?

2. Where does the story take place?

3. What time of year is it at the beginning of the chapter?

4. Who are the main people in Seka's family?

5. What do we learn about Seka's daily life?

6. What is the relationship between Seka and Zora?

7. What major event or conflict is introduced in this chapter?

8. How does Seka feel about their home?

9. What is the mood or atmosphere in the town at the start of the story?

**Inferential Questions**

1. Why does Seka describe her friendship with Zora as special?

2. What clues suggest that trouble is approaching for the town?

3. How does Seka's mother react to stress, and what does this tell us about her character?

4. Why do the adults seem tense or worried in this chapter?

5. How does the setting (the town, the school, the home) help establish the tone of the story?

6. Why does Seka's father talk about politics or war with the neighbours?

7. How do the small daily routines (like school and playing) contrast with the growing tension in the town?

8. What does Seka's relationship with Emir tell us about sibling bonds in difficult times?

**Critical Thinking and Connection Questions**

1. If you were in Seka's situation, how would you feel about the changes happening in the town?

2. Seka and Zora are from different ethnic backgrounds but remain close friends. What does this tell us about friendship during times of conflict?

3. Do you think Seka's family should have left their town earlier? Why or why not?

4. Why is it important to tell stories about historical events like this?

5. How does the first chapter make you feel? What emotions does the author create through the setting and character interactions?

6. Based on what you've read, what predictions can you make about what will happen next?

7. If you could ask Seka one question about her experiences, what would it be and why?

**Cloze Activity:**

**Word Bank:** abutted, chatter, corridors, unruly.

**Instructions:** Write the correct word in the blanks. Use the Word Bank for reference.

We walked the steep, curving road toward the centre of town and our high school. We were on afternoon shift, which began at one p.m. and finished at six p.m . The schoolhouse was a three-storey square white building that _____________________ a hill with the forest framing it from behind. The conifer trees were spiky and ____________________ as they covered the hill. I walked beside Zora onto the basketball court in front of the school, through the carpark, entering the front doorway. I climbed up the stairs to the third storey while students streamed ahead of us. The ___________________ echoed with the ____________________, and the squeaky shoes on linoleum filled the air.

**Sentence Structure Activity** – Identify the subject, verb, and object.

Zora and I ran up the hill behind our houses.

She handed me the white flower.

My father attempted to talk me into going to the mechanical high school.

Seka read from the romance novel.

Boris visited Seka's family late at night.

**Parts of Speech Identification** – Find nouns, verbs, adjectives, and adverbs in sentences.

The lush green trees covered the steep hill.

She quickly tucked the necklace under her shirt.

The dusty classroom smelled of old chalk.

He walked cautiously through the dark hallway.

They whispered nervously about the missing students.

**Punctuation and Capitalisation Activity** – Correct errors in given sentences.

zora and i ran up the hill behind our houses

he asked do you think we will find a love like that

mrs tanovic was already at her desk in the corner near the chalkboard

seka found a note that read why is everyone leaving

she whispered i dont want to leave

**Verb Tense Practice** – Fill in the missing word to convert sentences into past, present, and future tenses.

| Original | Past | Future |
|---|---|---|
| She reads the book in the trees. | She _____ the book in the trees. | She will read the book in the trees. |
| The students leave the classroom. | The students left the classroom. | The students ___ _____ the classroom. |
| Emir fights back against the bullies. | Emir _______ back against the bullies. | Emir will fight back against the bullies. |
| They sit together under the tree. | They sat together under the tree. | They _____________ together under the tree. |
| She whispers a secret to her friend. | She ___________ a secret to her friend. | She will whisper a secret to her friend. |

## CHAPTER 2

**Vocabulary Bank**

**Instructions:** Fill in the blanks with the correct word from the word bank below.

**Word Bank:**
Ultimatum – A final demand or statement of terms.

Camouflage – A pattern or colour that helps something blend into its surroundings.

Artillery – Large military guns used in warfare.

Encampment – A temporary settlement of people, especially soldiers or refugees.

Invasion – An attack by an army into another country or region.

Huddled – Crowded together in fear or cold.

Sinister – Giving the impression of something evil or dangerous.

Rummaged – Searched through something in a hurried way.

Foraged – Searched for food or supplies in the wild.

Looted – Stolen or taken by force.

**Sentences:**

The soldiers received an __________ to surrender or face the full force of the enemy army.

The military vehicle was covered in green and brown patterns to help it blend into the forest, providing effective __________.

The enemy forces were equipped with heavy __________, capable of causing massive damage from a long distance.

After a long march, the soldiers set up an __________ by the river, where they could rest and regroup.

The enemy's sudden __________ left the country's defences in chaos, and the citizens fled to safety.

The refugees __________ together for warmth as the cold wind howled through the camp.

There was something __________ about the abandoned mansion, like it held a dark secret.

The children __________ through the old attic, looking for forgotten treasures.

In the wilderness, the survivors __________ for berries and plants to sustain themselves.

After the town was attacked, the invaders __________ the homes, taking whatever they could find of value.

## Comprehension Questions

1. What were Emir and Seka doing when their father came home?

2. What news did Babo bring home?

3. Why did Mama panic when she tried to call her parents?

4. What signal did Seka use to communicate with Zora?

5. Where did the family take shelter when the Serbs started shelling?

6. What did Babo go upstairs to retrieve during the shelling?

7. How did Slobodan help the family?

8. Why did Seka's family have to hide in the woods?

9. What instructions did the family follow while escaping to the hill?

10. What made the camp in the woods difficult to live in?

**Inferential Questions**

1. How do we know that Babo was scared when he came home?

2. What does the basement symbolise for the family during the attack?

3. Why did Mama and Babo hesitate before deciding to hide in Slobodan's house?

4. What can you infer about Zora and Seka's friendship based on their goodbye?

5. How does Emir show that he is trying to take on more responsibility?

6. Why did people continue staying in their homes despite the danger?

7. What does the moment when Babo and Slobodan say goodbye reveal about their relationship?

8. How do we know that Slobodan's family truly cared for Seka's family?

**Critical Thinking and Connection Questions**

If you were in Seka's position, how would you have felt about trusting Slobodan's family?

**Parts of Speech Sort**

**Instructions:** Label the following words from the chapter into the correct category: **noun, verb, adjective, or adverb.**

| Word | Category |
| --- | --- |
| Cradle | |
| Shouted | |
| Despair | |
| Quickly | |
| Encampment | |
| Tremble | |
| Camouflage | |
| Huddled | |
| Sinister | |
| Barefoot | |

**Past Tense Transformation**

**Instructions:** Rewrite the following present-tense sentences in the past tense.

1. The Serbs **surround** the bus.

2. Mama **paces** around the house, looking worried.

3. Zora **takes** my hand in hers.

4. My father **lights** a cigarette and **inhales** deeply.

5. We **run** into the basement as the shells **fall**.

**Conjunctions Challenge**

**Instructions:** Fill in the blanks using **and, but, or, because, so.**

1. The family hid in the basement, _ _ _ _ _ they were afraid of the shelling.

2. Mama wanted to call her parents, _ _ _ _ _ the phone line was dead.

3. Emir was already taller than Babo, _ _ _ _ _ his coat only reached his knees.

4. The shelling stopped, _ _ _ _ _ the family still had to stay in hiding.

5. Seka felt exhausted, _ _ _ _ _ she still couldn't sleep properly.

### Adjective Hunt

**Instructions:** Find five adjectives in the following paragraph and underline them. Then, circle the noun each adjective describes.

### Paragraph:

The cold basement was dark and sinister, with shelves full of old blankets and dusty boxes. The weak light flickered, casting long shadows.

**Direct Speech Punctuation**

**Instructions:** Add correct punctuation to these direct speech sentences from the chapter.

1. what's happening I screamed as another explosion hit the house

2. come with me slobodan said

3. i'll never forget you I whispered to zora

4. let's go babo said We're going to be walking most of the night

5. salam aleikum my mother said

**Prepositions of Place**

**Instructions:** Fill in the blanks with the correct preposition: **under, in, on, beside, behind, between.**

1. The family hid ______ the basement during the attack.

2. Emir placed the wooden stove ______ the tree for protection.

3. Seka sat ______ Zora, holding her hand.

4. The gunfire came from the hills ______ the valley.

5. Slobodan's house was ______ theirs, making it easy to sneak over.

## CHAPTER 3

## Vocabulary Bank

| Word | Definition | Antonyms |
|---|---|---|
| Pariah | Someone who is rejected by society. | |
| Defector | Someone who leaves their country or group to join another. | |
| Despair | A deep feeling of hopelessness. | |
| Stoic | Remaining calm and strong in difficult times. | |
| Betrayal | A disloyal or harmful act against someone who trusts you. | |
| Grief | Deep sadness, especially after losing someone. | |
| Decimated | Destroyed or severely damaged. | |
| Traitor | Someone who betrays their country, friends, or group. | |

## Comprehension Questions

1. Why could Seka and Zora only read during the day-time?

2. What  did Babo do when the electricity was cut off?

3. What happened to Zora's house during the shelling?

4. How did Slobodan get injured?

5. Why did Slobodan and Petra move in to Boris' house instead of staying with the Seka's family?

6. What work was Babo drafted to do for the brigade?

7. Why isn't Slobodan allowed to volunteer for the brigade?

8. What did Seka and Emir see from Kalina Hill?

9. How did the refugees behave toward Zora's family?

10. Why did Zora's family decide to leave Srebrenica?

**Inferential Questions**

1. What does the way Zora reacts to her house being bombed tell us about her emotional state?

2. How do Slobodan's actions show his loyalty to Srebrenica despite being Serb?

3. Why do you think the soldiers used a megaphone to threaten Slobodan?

4. What do the descriptions of the destruction tell us about the intensity of the war?

5. How do the reactions of different people toward Zora's family show the impact of war on relationships?

6. Why does Emir choose to volunteer for the army, despite his father's wishes?

7. What does the moment when Seka holds her mother as she grieves tell us about their relationship?

8. How does the author create a sense of fear and tension in this chapter?

## Critical Thinking and Connection Questions

1. How do you think Zora felt when the refugees accused her family of being the enemy? How would you feel in her situation?

2. Do you agree with Slobodan's decision to stay in Srebrenica despite the danger? Why or why not?

3. Why do you think war makes people turn against their neighbours, even if they were once friends?

4. What do you think about Emir's decision to join the army? Would you have done the same in his place?

5. If you were Zora, would you want to leave for Australia, or would you try to stay? Explain your reasoning.

6. How does this chapter help us understand the way war affects friendships and families?

7. What are some ways people could help war refugees today to avoid situations like the ones described in this chapter?

**Parts of Speech Sort**

**Instructions:** Sort the following words from the chapter into the correct category: **noun, verb, adjective, or adverb.**

| Word | Category |
| --- | --- |
| Explosion | |
| Despair | |
| Trembling | |
| Destroyed | |
| Shattered | |
| Bravely | |
| Refugee | |
| Encircled | |
| Barricade | |
| Helpless | |

**Past Tense Transformation**

**Instructions:** Rewrite the following sentences in the past tense.

1. The Serbs **target** Slobodan's family.

2. Mama **caress** the photos of her parents.

3. The shells **destroy** Zora's house.

4. The refugees **loot** abandoned houses.

5. Zora **hold** my hand tightly as she said goodbye.

## Conjunctions Challenge

**Instructions:** Fill in the blanks using **and, but, or, because, so.**

1. The family stayed in the basement, _ _ _ _ _ they were afraid of another attack.

2. Slobodan wanted to fight, _ _ _ _ _ the soldiers didn't trust him.

3. The refugees searched the rubble, _ _ _ _ _ they found very little.

4. Mama tried to stay strong, _ _ _ _ _ she missed her parents deeply.

5. Zora's family moved away, _ _ _ _ _ it was too dangerous to stay.

## Adjective Hunt

**Instructions:** Find five adjectives in the following paragraph and underline them. Then, circle the noun each adjective describes.

**Paragraph:**
The frightened refugees searched through the ruined house, their tired faces filled with despair. The sharp smell of smoke still lingered in the air. A broken chair lay among the rubble, a reminder of the destruction.

**Direct Speech Punctuation**

**Instructions:** Add the correct punctuation to these direct speech sentences.

1. We need to go to the basement I said

2. Slobodan is a traitor the soldiers shouted through the megaphone

3. Let's go to your house tomorrow I suggested

4. I don't want to see the graveyard of my old life Zora whispered

5. You must not fall asleep Mama told Slobodan

**Prepositions of Place**

**Instructions:** Fill in the blanks with the correct preposition: **under, in, on, beside, behind, between.**

1. The family hid _ _ _ _ _ the basement during the attack.

2. Zora's family placed their belongings _ _ _ _ _ the back room.

3. A soldier stood _ _ _ _ _ the destroyed house, looking for movement.

4. Slobodan was injured and sat _ _ _ _ _ the wall to rest.

5. The refugees walked _ _ _ _ _ the abandoned houses, searching for items.

**Synonyms and Antonyms**

**Instructions:** Find the synonym and antonym for the words below.

| Word | Synonyms | Antonyms |
| --- | --- | --- |
| Destroyed | | |
| Afraid | | |
| Strong | | |
| Flee | | |
| Silent | | |

## CHAPTER 4

**Comprehension Questions**

1. Where did Seka and Zora go at the beginning of the chapter?

2. What was happening at the department store when they arrived?

3. Why was Zora's family unable to leave on the convoys?

4. How did Camouflage T-Shirt react when he found out Slobodan was Serb?

5. What distraction allowed Babo and Slobodan to escape from the soldier?

6. Who arrived at Seka's house later that day?

7. How did Seka react upon meeting Ramo for the first time?

8. Why did Ramo refuse to shake hands with Zora's family?

9. What did Zora and Seka decide to do to stay connected after she left?

10. Where was Zora's family planning to escape to?

## Inferential Questions

1. Why did Petra refuse to leave her older sons behind, even when she had the chance to escape?

2. What does the way Camouflage T-Shirt reacted to Slobodan tell us about growing ethnic divisions?

3. How does the way Babo handled the confrontation at the convoy show his leadership and quick thinking?

4. Why do you think Ramo reacted so negatively to Zora's family?

5. What does Seka's grandmother's appearance and exhaustion suggest about the journey she had taken?

6. How does the author use descriptions of food and coffee rituals to show life's contrast before and during the war?

7. How does Seka's fantasy about reuniting with Zora in Australia contrast with the reality of war?

## Critical Thinking and Connection Questions

1. What do you think about the way Ramo treated Zora? Should Seka have forgiven him? Why or why not?

2. How do you think the war changed people's relationships with their neighbours? Can you think of other examples in history where this happened?

3. Why do you think Seka and Zora created a notebook system to write to each other? Do you think it was a realistic way to stay connected?

4. How does the destruction of Seka's childhood village symbolise the loss of her innocence?

5. What are the dangers of ethnic divisions in communities? How can they be prevented?

6. Seka writes to Zora every day, even though she doesn't know if she will ever see her again. Why do you think she does this?

**Parts of Speech Sort**

**Instructions:** Label the following words from the chapter into the correct category: **noun, verb, adjective, or adverb.**

| Word | Category |
| --- | --- |
| Convoy | |
| Betrayal | |
| Persecuted | |
| Desperate | |
| Bravely | |
| Rootless | |
| Foraging | |
| Evacuate | |
| Prejudice | |
| Longing | |

**Past Tense Transformation**

**Instructions:** Rewrite the following sentences in the past tense.

1. The refugees **gather** at the department store.

2. Slobodan **try** to leave with his family.

3. Seka **hold** Zora's hand as they ran home.

4. Ramo **refuse** to shake hands with Zora.

5. The soldiers **block** the road, preventing their escape.

**Conjunctions Challenge**

**Instructions:** Fill in the blanks using **and, but, or, because, so.**

1. The soldier pointed his rifle at Slobodan, ______ Babo stepped in to protect him.

2. The convoy only allowed women and children, ______ Slobodan had to stay behind.

3. The refugees were exhausted, ______ they had no choice but to keep moving.

4. Seka wanted to stay with Zora, ______ she knew she had to say goodbye.

5. They needed to leave, ______ there were no more safe places left.

**Adjective Hunt**

**Instructions:** Find five adjectives in the following paragraph and underline them. Then, circle the noun each adjective describes.

**Paragraph:**

The desperate refugees gathered at the crowded department store, waiting for their turn. The panicked soldier waved his rifle in the air. A nervous mother held onto her child, watching the looming trucks that would take them away.

**Direct Speech Punctuation**

**Instructions:** Add the correct punctuation to these direct speech sentences.

1. You can't leave without your family Slobodan said

2. I will never forgive you Ramo Seka whispered

3. We need to escape tonight Zora's father explained

4. I will find you one day  Seka promised

5. Let's hurry before someone stops us Babo urged

**Prepositions of Place**

**Instructions:** Fill in the blanks with the correct preposition: **under, in, on, beside, behind, between.**

1. The refugees hid _ _ _ _ _ the trees, waiting for darkness.

2. Zora's notebook was tied _ _ _ _ _ her waist.

3. The soldier stood _ _ _ _ _ the truck, checking for more people.

4. Seka walked _ _ _ _ _ her father, holding his hand tightly.

5. The enemy soldiers were stationed _ _ _ _ _ the hills, watching the town.

**Synonyms and Antonyms**

**Instructions:** Find the synonym and antonym for the words below.

| Word | Synonym | Antonym |
|---|---|---|
| Desperate | | |
| Safe | | |
| Hope | | |
| Betrayal | | |
| Protect | | |

# DOWNLOAD

## TEACHING RESOURCES
## ANSWER KEY

https://www.amrapajalic.com/tree.html

# Note about the novel

This novel is a work of historical fiction inspired by real events. To ensure authenticity and honour the experiences of those who lived through this period, I relied on first-hand accounts and survivor stories. These powerful narratives provided invaluable insight into the human cost of war and the resilience of those who endured it. The following books were instrumental in my research and served as essential resources for recreating the world and events depicted in this story. A more comprehensive bibliography is available in my book of essays *Fragments of History: The Essays Behind the Stories*.

**Research Sources:**

Clark, T. R. (2014). *The United Nations Peacekeepers and Local Population of the United Nations Safe Area Srebrenica: (De) Construction of Human Relationships*. Nova Gorica: University of Nova Gorica Graduate School.

Filipović, Zlata. (2006). *Zlata's Diary: A Child's Life in Wartime Sarajevo, Revised Edition*. New York: Penguin Books.

Fink, Sheri. (2003). *War Hospital: A True Story of Surgery and Survival*. New York: PublicAffairs.

Hasanović, Hasan. (2016). *Surviving Srebrenica*. Aberdeenshire: Lumphanan Press.

Gutman, R. (1993a). *A witness to genocide: The first inside account of the horrors of "ethnic cleansing" in Bosnia*. Macmillan.

Leydesdorff, Selma. (2015). *Surviving the Bosnian Genocide: The Women of Srebrenica Speak*. Bloomington: Indiana University Press.

Nuhanović, Hasan. (2019). *The Last Refuge: A True Story of War, Survival and Life Under Siege in Srebrenica* (M. Evtov & A. Sluiter, Trans.). London: Peter Owen Publishers.

Rohde, David. (2012). *Endgame: The Betrayal and Fall of Srebrenica, Europe's Worst Massacre Since World War II*. New York: Penguin Books.

Sacco, Joe. (2018). *Safe Area Goražde: The War in Eastern Bosnia 1992–1995*. Seattle: Fantagraphics Books.

Sekulić, Midhat. (2014). *Srebrenica: Massacre on School Playground*. DW. Retrieved March 25, 2019, from .

Sells, M. A. (1996). *The bridge betrayed: Religion and genocide in Bosnia*. University of California Press.

Sudetić, Chuck. (1998). *Blood and Vengeance: One Family's Story of the War in Bosnia* (1st ed.). New York: W. W. Norton & Co.

Suljagić, Emir. (2005). *Postcards from the Grave*. London: Saqi Books.

Willem, J., & Both, N. (1996). *Srebrenica: Record of a war crime*. London: Penguin Books.

*Fragments of History: The Essays Behind the Stories*

If you're interested in learning more about the historical context of Srebrenica and the research that informed this novel, I have compiled a companion collection of essays titled *Fragments of History: TheEssays Behind the Stories.*

This book is not commercially available and is offered exclusively to my newsletter subscribers. You can sign up at www.amrapajalic.com

## Acknowledgment

I would like to express my deepest gratitude to the survivors who have shared their stories, both in books and through interviews. Their courage in recounting such painful memories has allowed future generations to bear witness to the truth and understand the enduring impact of these events. This novel is dedicated to them, as well as to all those who were silenced by war and genocide.

# Seka Torlak Series

*Forged on the war-torn streets of Srebrenica, Seka Torlak fights for justice, retribution and truth.*

**Book 1: Time Kneels Between Mountains**

*Srebrenica, 1992*

*In a town where survival is a daily battle, there are those who seek justice...*

Overnight, Seka Torlak's life as a regular teenager is up-ended as Srebrenica, her once peaceful town, falls under siege and she faces starvation, shelling, and sniper attacks. When desperately needed antibiotics and food disappear and are sold on the black market, Seka vows to investigate the corruption and bring the culprits to justice.

As the war ravages Srebrenica, Seka's resilience is tested as she navigates loss, fear, and the harsh realities of war. Yet, amidst the devastation, she finds a glimmer of hope as her relationship with Ramo blossoms from friendship to love.But as she fights for justice and love, will Seka triumph, or will the brutal war tear everything she holds dear apart?

*Bonus Short Story: Belma's Liberation*

*In a village shadowed by abuse, there are those with courage who fight for liberation...*

Sign up to my newsletter and read *Belma's Liberation* to find out how Seka saved her from her abusive father

**Book 2: Ghosts Among the Gumtrees**

*Melbourne, 1997*

*In a city where the guilty roam free, there are those who seek retribution...*

After surviving the brutal siege of Srebrenica, Seka Torlak is trying to rebuild her life as a refugee in Melbourne, 1997. But her fragile peace is shattered when she spots a war criminal responsible for her father's death walking freely in the city. Determined to uncover his true identity and bring him to justice, Seka delves into an investigation that reveals a sinister underbelly of suburbia, where genocide deniers hide in plain sight.

Haunted by memories of war and loss, Seka grapples with the raging conflict within her: the pursuit of justice versus the thirst for retribution. As she navigates this perilous path, she must decide what she is willing to sacrifice for the truth. Will Seka find her salvation, or will she lose her soul in the process?

*Bonus Short Story: Zora's Story*

*In the ruins of war, there are those who cling to memories of friendship...*

Sign up to my newsletter and read *Zora's Story* to find out her story in escaping the war.

**Book 3: Mad Dawn Winter**

*Riverwood, 1998*

*In a town submerged with secrets and corruption, there are those who seek the truth...*

Seka Torlak, now a journalism cadet, relocates to the tranquil town of Riverwood in 1998, seeking a fresh start. However, her peace is short-lived when she stumbles upon a cold case involving the murder of a formerVietnam Vet. Driven by a grieving mother's plea for justice, Seka begins to uncover a web of secrets that this seemingly idyllic town has buried deep.

In her quest for truth, Seka befriends Dawn Winter, a fellow Bosnian woman haunted by the loss of a friend and ostracised by the townspeople for her tributes to the fallen. As Seka digs deeper, she finds herself entangled in a dangerous game of deceit and loyalty, facing ghosts of the past and present. Will she unravel the truth and deliver justice before it's too late, or will the town's dark secrets consume her?

*Bonus Short Story: Art's War*

*In a time of loss and grief, there are those who pursue the truth...*

Sign up to my newsletter and read *Art's Fall* to find out about his investigation first-hand

*Bonus Short Story: The Regrets of Ben Hayes*
*In a war where fear reigns, love remains unspoken...*

Sign up to my newsletter and read *The Regrets of Ben Hayes* to find out about his first love during his service as a National Serviceman

# BONUS CONTENT

## SHORT STORY
## HISTORICAL RESEARCH ESSAYS
## TEACHING RESOURCES

https://www.amrapajalic.com/seka-torlak-series.html

# BONUS CONTENT

**A powerful reckoning with memory, identity, and survival.**

*Fragments of History* uncovers the hidden truths behind the Srebrenica genocide—from the silencing of Muslim identity to the weaponisation of Islamophobia and the myth of Yugoslav unity. Through deeply personal and sharply analytical essays, it honours the resilience of Bosniak women and preserves the voices history tried to erase.

https://www.amrapajalic.com/seka-torlak-series.html

# About the author

Amra Pajalic is an award-winning Australian author, educator, and indie publisher known for crafting compelling stories that blend heart, humour, and heritage. Her work explores themes of identity, belonging, and resilience, often drawing from her Bosnian background. She won the 2009 Melbourne Prize for Literature's Civic Choice Award for her debut novel The Good Daughter, re-released as Sabiha's Dilemma (Pishukin Press, 2022). The anthology she co-edited, Growing up Muslim in Australia (Allen and Unwin, 2014), was shortlisted for the 2015 Children's Book Council of the year awards and her memoir Things Nobody Knows But Me (Transit Lounge, 2019) was shortlisted for the 2020 National Biography Award. Her short story collection The

Cuckoo's Song (Pishukin Press) features previously published and prize-winning stories.

Amra is the author of the Sassy Saints series, a young adult contemporary  trilogy set in Melbourne's western suburbs. These stories feature  smart-mouthed teens, love triangles, fake friends, and fierce girl power,  offering a refreshing take on multicultural Australian life.

She is also the creator of the gripping Seka Torlak crime mystery series.  Forged on the war-torn streets of Srebrenica, Seka Torlak fights for justice,  retribution and truth.

Amra is committed to accessibility and inclusion in publishing. Through her  micro-press, Pishukin Press, she releases her titles in a wide range of  formats—including audiobook, large print, dyslexic font, paperback, ebook,  and hardback—to ensure all readers can experience her stories.

When she's not writing, Amra is podcasting on Amra's Armchair Anecdotes,  mentoring emerging writers, and delivering workshops across Australia on  self-publishing, writing craft, and creative resilience.

Amra Pajalić also publishes romance novels under pen name Mae Archer.

g   goodreads.com/author/show/3310015.Amra_Pajalic

f   facebook.com/AmraPajalicAuthor/

instagram.com/amrapajalicauthor/

https://twitter.com/AmraPajalic

tiktok.com/@amrapajalic

youtube.com/c/AmraPajalicAuthor

**SIGN UP FOR AMRA'S AUTHOR NEWSLETTER**

For news, giveaways, bonus material, and sneak peeks, please sign up to her newsletter below.

www.amrapajalic.com

**Help Bring the *Seka Torlak* Series to Life—Your Reviews Matter!**

Dear Reader,

Thank you for reading a novel in the *Seka Torlak* series—a gripping story of justice, survival, and resilience set against the backdrop of war. This series is deeply personal, shaped by years of research and a passion for shedding light on untold histories.

Now, I need *your* help. Reviews are the lifeblood of independent authors like me. They help spread the word, connect the right readers with the book, and ensure this series reaches as many people as possible. If you've read my novels, I'd love to hear your thoughts!

A few sentences about what connected with you—whether it's Seka's journey, the historical depth, or the emotional impact—can make a world of difference. You can leave your rating and/or review on the website you purchased the book from.

Your support means everything. Thank you for being part of this journey with me.

*Hvala lijepo*/Much thanks,
**Amra Pajalić**

# Also by

**Seka Torlak Series**
The Tree That Stood Still
Time Kneels Between Mountains
Ghosts Among the Gumtrees
Mad Dawn Winter

**Memoir**
Things Nobody Knows But Me
Growing up Muslim in Australia

**Sassy Saints Series**
Sabiha's Dilemma
Alma's Loyalty
Jesse's Triumph

**Young Adult**
The Cuckoo's Song
The Climb

**Romance as Mae Archer**
Return to Me
Hollywood Dreams

Vintage Dreams

## Dark Fiction/Horror as A.P. Pajalic

Woman on the Edge